LESSONS & LOVERS

by

PORTIA DA COSTA

LESSONS AND LOVERS
Copyright © 2013/2016 by Portia Da Costa
Cover Art Design © Portia Da Costa
Cover and Interior Layout by Croco Designs

This story is a work of fiction. The names, characters, places, and incidents are products of the writer's imagination or have been used fictitiously and are not to be construed as real. Any resemblance to persons, living or dead, actual events, locales or organizations is entirely coincidental.

All rights reserved. With exception of quotes used in reviews, this story may not be reproduced or used in whole or in part by any means existing without written permission from the author.

Please be aware that this story contains sensual content that is only suitable for adult readers who are comfortable with frank language and descriptions of erotic scenarios. LESSONS AND LOVERS is an escapist erotic fantasy. If they existed in the real world, my characters would always use condoms.

LESSONS AND LOVERS was originally published digitally by Ellora's Cave.

Chapter One

The night was humid. Damp flesh slapped and smacked as belly met belly in a savage, primeval rhythm. Sweat dripped into Hettie's eyes and coated her skin like a sheen of raw silk. It was almost a relief when the telephone trilled.

But it wasn't really. Not when she needed to come, and come hard. She died inside as Starr paused in the middle of a thrust and looked down at her solemnly. He was the perfect servant in her bed now, his eyes cool and shuttered. The lover had gone as if he'd never existed, and a clutch of vague, unspoken hopes had shattered in Hettie's heart. Her body still burned, but she felt like wailing out in loss.

"Are you going to answer that, ma'am?" His voice was as calm as a lake, his composure unruffled. Even the slide of his flesh pulling out of hers couldn't disturb his complete *sangfroid*.

So detached. Even now, thought Hettie, swallowing her disappointment.

"I suppose so," she replied, easing herself from beneath his long, golden body.

Why, oh why, did this have to happen? Who the hell

was calling at this time? Didn't they have anything better to do than destroy the first step in her recovery? Destroy her chance to...

Chance to do what, Hettie? To understand your feelings for Starr? And his for you?

What if he doesn't have any? Other than duty and respect and loyalty. And desire, obviously.

What if, by asking him, she screwed up what she *could* have with him? Which was amazing sex. On demand. Whenever she wanted it.

And tonight was the first time since Piers' death that she had wanted it. The first time her healthy woman's body had tingled and finally come alive again. The first time she'd wanted to feel a man's stiffness moving inside her. The long gliding stroke of a cock to make her feel she was wholly and completely female.

It had been months, and yet somehow Starr had known that tonight she'd been ready at last. Without any word or prior indication, he'd come to her bed, then silently and gracefully, he'd slid between the sheets beside her and started touching her with his unique, almost surgical precision.

Not one word had passed his lips as he'd cupped her firm breasts and delicately kneaded them. Not one sound as he'd slid his stroking hand over her flat belly and her hips. Not a murmur had he uttered. Even as his fingers had parted the lips of her sex and played in the thick, clinging moisture they'd found there. It was only as he'd pressed open her slim thighs and entered her that he'd spoken, only as he'd possessed that he'd whispered her name. Called her "Hettie", as he only ever had done when his cock was sheathed in her body.

Her hunger had flared, that sense of being completely alive doubling and redoubling as her sex had quickened and gripped him. She'd cried out, riding his thrusts on the crest of a great, wet wave of erotic energy.

But it had been more than just fucking, and the feelings much deeper. Her heart had leapt as her body had responded. She'd felt something fragile and beautiful unfurling that went far beyond sex. Some tenuous and unspoken emotional conduit being formed between herself and the man making love to her.

And then the bedside telephone had shattered the spell, and her fragile hopes and dreams.

"The phone, ma'am," he prompted.

"All right already! I'm answering it!" she snapped, the moment lost as his semen cooled on her naked thighs, "but for God's sake, Starr, don't make a sound!"

"Of course, ma'am," Starr answered mildly.

Hettie felt small and mean. She'd snarled at him without justification, in the middle of a moment that was at least *physically* intimate. For all his emotional impenetrability, Starr had always been gentle, caring and attentive. Both in bed and in the course of his more conventional duties. And he was glorious too! Hettie's reborn libido stirred like a serpent in her loins as her companion levered himself up and showed her the perfect, gilded breadth of his back and the tight muscular rounds of his supremely male ass. Turning to the small bedside table, he reached for the handset and lifted it with almost supernatural quietness.

With the same almost uncanny lack of fuss, he handed it to her then slid elegantly away and sat on the edge of the bed.

Hettie scooted across the rumpled sheet and settled herself against the pillows, thankful only that her late-night caller couldn't see her. See that she was naked and obviously fresh from sex. Her gold-blonde hair was a mess, her usually pale face and body all flushed and her eyes overbright. Her mouth was bruised from kissing and she frowned as she held the receiver close to it.

Conversation was going to be difficult. It was well-nigh impossible to think about anything but Starr and his sleek naked body. His pose was utterly relaxed, even though his cock was still glistening and stiff. His erection seemed harder than ever.

"Goddammit!" mimed Hettie, then cautiously said, "Hello?"

"Good evening," said the smooth yet accented voice of an operator, "I have a call for Lady Henrietta Miller from *Signorina* Renata di Angeli in Milan. Shall I put it through?"

Renata! Oh, what now?

With Ren it could only be a crisis. Hettie shuffled her pillows against the padded headboard and stretched out her long, shapely legs in Starr's direction. Better get comfy because this could take some time. Her foot touched a warm well-muscled thigh and she shivered involuntarily as he looked around, his expression inquiring.

"Yes, put it through, please," Hettie said to the distant operator, but as Starr placed his fingers on her calf and smoothed them lightly up towards her knee and the creamy under-slope of her thigh, she was suddenly less interested in Renata's latest catalog of troubles.

"Hettie! Hettie! I'm so sorry! I know it's late and stuff but I had to talk to you!" cried a familiar voice on the phone.

"Don't worry. I was awake anyway." Hettie suddenly couldn't think of a thing to say to her friend as Starr's hand stole higher and higher in search of hotter and damper zones. "I couldn't sleep so I was reading. But never mind me, Ren. What's happened? Even *you* don't call me in the middle of the night for nothing!"

"Oh, Hett, I'm in an awful mess! You've got to help me!"

LESSONS & LOVERS

the distant voice wailed. "You're the only one!"

"It's a man, isn't it?"

It mostly was in Renata's case, and under normal circumstances Hettie would have listened attentively. But Starr's long, golden hand was stroking the tender borderline between her thigh and her trembling pussy now, and each lingering pass was getting closer and closer to the place that still longed for him.

"Yes, Hett, it is! Well, two of them actually. And I'm going to lose one if I don't get rid of the other! Well, not really, because there's nothing between us. It's just that Fausto won't stay if Darryl does! Oh, Hettie, I don't know what to do! You're the only one who can help me!" Furious sobbing burst from the receiver as Renata succumbed to tears in the way she so often did.

Hettie let her friend cry. Not out of cruelty, but because she felt that she might break down herself any second. Lose control and moan because her lover was kneeling between her thighs now, crouched in the space he'd created by grasping her ankles and stretching them wide apart. His own thighs bracketed his swaying erection, while his vivid blue gaze was riveted on her rudely displayed crotch.

Hettie felt herself twitch and sizzle. He was caressing her as surely with his laser-beam eyes as he did with his nimble fingers. As surely as he'd done earlier when he'd first explored the sleeping vale of her sex. After her extended celibacy since Piers' death, she'd sensed that Starr felt he had to prepare her properly. Ready her with skill and exquisite tenderness, with a slow rhythmic rubbing across the tender membranes and the straining, swelling bud...

"Hettie! You're not listening!" Renata cried woefully.

"Yes I am!" gasped Hettie, as Starr leaned forward and laid his long, slender-fingered hand lightly on her palpitating belly. His touch was so controlled it was barely there, yet it transferred itself directly to her open, yearning sex. Without conscious volition, her hips rose to invite him. A cry of need bubbled in her throat and she stopped it by biting her knuckle.

"Hettie!" Renata protested.

"Yes, but look, Ren, I don't know what you're talking about! Who are all these men?" Voice control was difficult now. Starr had a finger in the sticky, darkened mat of her pubic hair and was twirling and gently tugging. "Tell me what's happened. Tell me it all, then maybe I can help." She closed her eyes. Maybe she could manage to listen if she couldn't see? See what was happening to her. See Starr's marvelous body. His heavy but beautiful cock... His bright blue eyes boring into her as his hands made her writhe with pleasure.

"All right." There was a sound of rustling and snuffling. Renata wrestling with tears. "I've been seeing this man. He's moved into the palazzo. His name's Fausto and it's so good between us... *Really* good! I have orgasms with him, Hett, and you know how hard it is for me."

Oh my God!

Hettie's teeth closed harder on her knuckles as Starr pushed two fingers slowly into her. *Ren can't come and I can hardly stop myself!* She remembered their no-holds-barred girlie chats, and how she'd always had to play down the fact that she could climax so easily. Especially with the man in her bed right now.

I bet Starr could bring you off, Ren! Helplessly, she jerked beneath his expert caress.

This could get to any woman. Two fingers moved wetly between her labia. Splitting around her clitoris, they teased her trembling pussy without ever touching the most crucial point of all. That he *didn't* touch it was almost unbearable. It took a superhuman effort to carry on listening.

"We were getting on like a dream. I even thought... I even thought he might propose or something. And then Darryl arrived!"

"Darryl?" inquired Hettie faintly. Inside she was screaming and begging. Begging harder than Ren had ever done for anything. Ready to plead with Starr that he touch his tapered fingertip to her clitoris.

"He's a sort of cousin of mine. Step-cousin really. I'm not sure. He's only half Italian. He was adopted by my Uncle Alfredo, but I never knew he existed until now. They were out excavating at some archaeological dig or other and there was an accident. A slide or rockfall or something... Uncle Alfredo was killed but Darryl escaped with minor injuries. Apart from losing his memory from a knock on the head, that is. Partially... He knows who he is, but not much else. And the hospital sent him to me! I'm his only relative, they say, because Aunt Maria died years ago, and there is nobody else. He's spent all his life in this monklike existence miles from civilization, just digging for relics and stuff with Uncle Alfredo and but now he's got to learn to live with other people."

Renata started sobbing again. Hettie wanted to ask what was wrong now, but at that second Starr gave in to her. He settled one finger on her clitoris, rubbed gently but firmly, and Hettie started sobbing too. Only her abused fist masked the sound. When his finger swirled, then pressed again, it was too much. Her loins churned and her sex pulsed like a heartbeat. Pleasure flared hot and sweet in her besieged clitoris, and she heard Renata wail incoherently, as if by proxy, her voice unknowingly proclaiming her friend's orgasm.

It was a few moments before either of them could speak—for their so vastly different reasons—but as she relaxed, still panting slightly, it was Hettie who managed first. As Starr slid up to her side and took her into his arms.

"Are you all right, Ren? What's wrong? What's so awful about your cousin?"

"There's nothing wrong with him," Renata gulped. "He's nice, really. But he's hanging around...*looking* at me all the time. As if he's waiting for something. Waiting for me to tell him things. I don't know. It's as if he wants me to *educate* him somehow... Help him remember everything. And... I mean..."

"Mean what, Ren, what?" urged Hettie. Her own immediate turmoil over, she felt worried about her confused friend. Poor Ren had no Starr to manage her problems for her. No elegant, athletic blond servant to lie beside her, hold her glowing post-orgasmic body and smooth his sex-scented hand gently over her sweaty, tousled hair.

"It's awkward, Hett. Darryl's...er...twenty-two... or twenty-three, I think. But he still seems quite innocent somehow. He looks at me. You know...*that* sort of look! It's as if he wants to be taught about...about sex and stuff!"

It was all wrong to laugh, but Hettie couldn't help herself. Mirth bubbled in her throat, and sharp-eared Starr, who'd obviously heard the other woman's shrill voice, laid his hand lightly over his mistress's mouth to stop her giggling. She could taste herself on his fingers and her sex twitched in response. It took several moments to suppress both amusement and desire.

Renata had a very strange dilemma.

"Sexuality goes deeper than memory, Ren. He can't have forgotten what sex is!"

It sounded preposterous, and yet maybe there was a

grain of truth in what she'd just said. For so long she'd felt neutered by her own grief. Both physically and emotionally. Mourning Piers, she'd forgotten what lust felt like and her feelings had been bound up, as if in a closed box. She, who'd always lusted and laughed and had so much love to give. Maybe this unknown Darryl had also been traumatized like that?

Ren's next words confirmed her theory.

"Oh he has! I'm sure he has! And I wouldn't mind telling him things. Being kind of like an aunt or something. But Fausto won't have it! He doesn't want Darryl around, and he certainly doesn't want me giving him sex education lessons!"

She fell silent and Hettie got an ominous feeling in the pit of her stomach. Starr's barely perceptible nod said he was coming to the same conclusions as she was.

"Ren? What's all this leading up to?" It was a pointless question. Any idiot could work out what was coming next.

"Well, Fausto's cleared off and he says he's not coming back until Darryl's out of the palazzo." She paused, and though Hettie couldn't see her, she knew her friend was gathering herself. "I was wondering if Darryl could come and stay with you a while? I know it's a bad time. But maybe some different company would be good for you! You must be lonely in that great big place all on your own. Oh, I know there's Starr. But he's so... Well, he's so sort of formal, and detached, and hung up on mistress and servant protocol and stuff, isn't he?"

Hettie looked up. Starr was leaning over her now, his face as calm as ever, his chiseled but generous mouth curving in the faintest of smiles. He eased a lock of hair from her brow, then smoothed the whole long, damp golden mass of it reverently across the pillow. His mouth touched hers, kissing her slightly off-center to avoid the telephone. His fingers closed on her breast, felt the hard-peaking nipple then tensed slightly. Hettie knew, with a shiver of delight, that he'd soon be inside her again.

How does this fit into mistress and servant protocol? she wondered for perhaps the thousandth time, feeling a breath-catching twist in her heart that was dangerously unrelated to the sex.

"What do you think, Hett?" persisted Renata, dissolving the fleeting thought, "Can Darryl come and stay with you? He's quiet, but he's actually quite charming in his own way. And he speaks perfect English. Really! And you've got all those filthy books in Piers' collection that he can read. He can do his learning and his sex revision from them, can't he?"

There was desperate hope in Renata's voice, and Hettie looked to Starr for help. Only if he approved, would she take in Ren's shy charmer. Her cool blond servant regarded her steadily for a few seconds, then took her hand and kissed it. When he looked up again, he nodded.

"Okay, Ren! He can stay for a while."

"Oh, thank you, Hett! Thank you! Thank you! Thank you! I love you! I knew you'd help me!"

"All right! Don't go overboard! Just one thing, though." Starr was kissing her again now, his lips warm and drifting on her bare, rounded breast. "Can the arrangements wait until tomorrow? I'm…um… Well, I'm starting to actually feel quite drowsy now and I'd like to get some sleep." It was a white lie, but she was entitled to it.

She gnawed her lip as Starr sucked roughly at her nipple, biting it slightly. She couldn't talk to Ren much longer, not while this beautiful torture was going on! There was no way she could suppress the screams of another orgasm.

"Oh yes, of course! Everything will be fine now!" Ren's voice was buoyant, "I'll call Fausto. He'll come back when he knows Darryl's leaving. Everything will be wonderful now! Thanks again, sweetheart, you've saved my life. I'll call you tomorrow. Bye, Hett! Sleep tight!"

"Goodnight, Ren!" said Hettie on a long broken gasp. As the connection died, Starr's fingers slid back between her sticky thighs. And the magic torment began all over again.

Dropping the lifeless receiver, Hettie tried to caress his sex in return, but he guided her hand away before she could even lay one finger on his stiffness.

"This is for you alone, milady." His voice was muffled, the words tangled around her nipple as he sucked and sucked and sucked.

But I want more!

Fighting for coherent thought, Hettie pushed at Starr's shoulder and made him lift his head.

"Let me touch you. Let me do something for you. It's what I want."

A strange, complicated expression passed across his astonishing face, then with a wry twist of his lips and a slight shrug, he reached for her hand and put it upon him.

The miracle of Starr's cock never ceased to amaze her. He was so hard, and yet the skin there was fine and delicate as satin. He stirred in her hand and seemed to grow harder than ever, if that were possible. As she gave him a slow, exploratory squeeze, his eyelashes fluttered and his lips parted in a stifled gasp.

For one frozen moment in time, Hettie almost seemed to feel Starr's pleasure. It was as if he were allowing her into his male mind and showing her what her touch did to him.

But the intimate communion was over almost as soon as it had begun.

"Enough, milady," he whispered, gently but firmly putting her hand from his flesh, then bending over her and taking her nipple between his lips once more.

And now each pull on her breast seemed to pull on her clitoris too, seemed to pass right through her struggling body and meet the gentle petting finger between her legs. Pinned between two nodes of pleasure, she could only thrash and moan. Tearing at the sheets beneath her, she soared to first one excruciating climax, then another and another and another.

"Thank you, Starr! Oh thank you, thank you, thank you!" she chanted in time to the pulsations that rippled through her. The sensations were sublime, and yet, even in the midst of them, her mind longed for something more, something different. She had no intimate name, no romantic lover's name with which to praise this incredible man who was so close to her, yet more distant than the stars he was named for. He had never offered a first name, and there was something so remote about him—even now!—that still made her afraid to ask.

Orgasming continuously, she babbled and raved, and her obedient demon switched to a different assault. Two fingers went deep, deep inside her, sliding easily into her buttery flesh and curving deftly to press against her G-spot.

One firm touch there and she was screaming and kicking her legs, her bottom bouncing high off the sweat-soaked sheet.

But Starr would not be shaken from his target. Or his infernal internal stroking.

"Please," she begged hoarsely, not even knowing whether it was for less contact, or for more. Her fingers flew to her jumping clitoris. To meet *his* caressing finger at her body's most exquisite nexus.

She was still rubbing when she felt his hand withdraw and his mouth leave her breast. She whimpered with loss, but the cries were wildly premature. Within moments, his cock filled the void inside her and his firm lips were covering her mouth.

She sobbed silently as their breaths mingled. A kiss was somehow closer, more joined even, than the sex. If he could kiss her so sweetly, it must mean that he cared for her in some deeper way? As he began to fuck her, she worked her clitoris greedily in time to his thrusts. The combined stimuli were deliciously wicked. Each time he plunged deep, her fingers were jammed against her flesh. It was a double pleasure. A double fuck. And in moments she was coming again, the orgasm doubly strong.

"Starr!" she keened as her body seemed to dissolve and reform, her complicated emotions calmed, for the moment, by simple uncomplicated pleasure. Grief for her late husband, confused guilt, frustrated longing to touch the heart of the man inside her…all were soothed by the power of magnificently satisfying sex. "Starr!" she sobbed, smiling beneath his lips as a warm flow bathed her pussy, his thick rush of semen a balm for all her ills.

His own orgasm was intense, staccato, almost animalistic, and on the last thrust, he collapsed and sighed heavily into her neck. It was just a long exhausted exhalation, but at the very limits of her hearing, Hettie knew she'd heard her own name.

"Oh, Starr, that was beautiful!" she murmured, winding her arms around him, trying to crush every inch of herself against his damp, hard, muscle-packed form.

But he gently pried her off again.

"Let me up, ma'am. I'm too heavy. I don't want to squash you," he whispered, shaking himself free and lying down—long, golden and magnificent—beside her.

"What if I want to be squashed?" she replied, drowsily

resigning herself to being "ma'am" once more.

It was no use taking him to task about that again. She couldn't be upset or angry with him after the beauty he'd just made for her. The way he'd lifted her from the pit and made life bright again. Badgering him about what he called her—either while they fucked, or at all other times—made not one iota of difference. He was as intransigent about her name as he was about his. Starr was always, always "Starr", and Hettie was only "Hettie" when he had his cock lodged deep inside her.

Which it wasn't now, so she was "milady" as she curled up alongside him and got the warmth of his strong arm around her shoulders, drawing him against her. She was tired now, really tired, but as she started to drift, stray thoughts popped into her head.

What was she going to do about Darryl? She'd agreed to take him in, and yet the presence of another man in the house would only make the task of understanding her relationship with Starr more complicated.

Without thinking, she sighed, and as she did so, she felt Starr's grip on her tighten infinitesimally, as he sensed her tension.

Why now? She knew even as she thought it that there really was no other choice. *Heaven knows, I know enough about grief and confusion and loneliness... How can I deny the poor man a refuge?*

We'll just have to go on as we are a bit longer, Starr, she told her servant silently, instinctively pressing her cheek to the warm cushion of his muscular chest. She'd so longed to breach this beautiful man's barrier of formality, and find out if the locked-down feelings she sensed—and prayed for—in him were as real as she hoped them to be. As real as hers were, she acknowledged in sudden astonishment, shocked at first, then in her mind seeing her late husband's smile of impish approval.

Oh Piers, what's happening to me? Is it really possible to love two men at once?

She'd loved her husband, really loved him, but she knew he would have been the first person to encourage her to seek love again. And perhaps even put forward his choice for the recipient of her love. God knows, the two men had been as much friends as employer and employee. Within the bounds of Starr's strict adherence to protocol, of course…

For a long while, her thoughts circulated around and around, touching on Starr, Piers and occasionally the mysterious Darryl. But finally, and mercifully, all her anxieties began to melt and become formless in the face of sheer exhaustion, and she surrendered to the comfort of the living pillow of Starr's chest.

When she woke the next morning, Hettie felt unexpectedly refreshed and at peace with the world. Despite the troubled whirl of her thoughts before sleep, she sensed, in the optimistic light of day, that some sort of progress had been made. She and Starr had been physically intimate again, and that was one step closer. Closer to the goal she sensed her heart wanted, and that every instinct told her that Piers would have wanted for her too.

"I'm think I'm getting better now, old thing," she murmured softly, talking to her reflection in the mirror as much as to her dead husband. "I really think I'm going to be okay soon. I've just got to go for it, haven't I?"

Piers would've been delighted, she knew, to see her eyes

looking brilliantly sparkling again. And to recognize the glossy sheen that only comes from superlative sex overlaying her smooth pale skin.

The most radical proof of recovery though was actually thinking about Piers without pain. She missed her dead husband, of course, but now she could think about the rest of her life, and what, and who, she wanted in it. She could remember the good times with Piers, but she could also believe in the possibility of better ones to come.

Especially now Starr was back in her bed performing his "special" duties. The ones he'd begun when Piers had become too ill to make love. The strong, quiet blond had been a sort of combination of personal assistant, concierge, bodyguard and chauffeur throughout the whole of the short Miller marriage, but in the last few months of it, sexual surrogacy had been added to his multifunction role.

Hettie had said nothing about Piers' reduced libido at first. His gentle lovemaking, his clever hands, and his experienced, exploring mouth had always given her immense pleasure and made her climax repeatedly. Even if their sex sessions hadn't been that frequent. But as a woman with generous erotic appetite, she soon became painfully frustrated as the gaps between those interludes became longer and longer and longer.

She had taken up horseback riding. She'd swum twice, three times a day. She'd started a rigorous aerobics program. And she'd masturbated in every private moment she could grab, rubbing her pussy with a frantic desperation that'd often made her sore but rarely eradicated her need. She'd even tried therapy. And though it'd been good to talk to someone about her frustration, talking could do nothing for the fires that burned in her sex.

And as Piers had become weaker, she'd simply lain next

to him, letting him hold her close while she'd stroked her own pussy and given herself the orgasms her fit young body demanded. She'd not complained, because she'd loved him so much and there was a certain sweetness to masturbating in his arms. For Piers' part, just to be there when she climaxed seemed to make him happy.

Then one night he'd said, "This isn't enough for you, my love, is it?"

She'd protested vehemently.

"It is, Piers! It is! I love you, darling! Fucking isn't everything. I knew what the deal was when we married. I married you for yourself, not your sexual performance." She touched his dear, gaunt face and looked into his weary eyes, trying to convince him. It *was* the truth. She missed full-on, hard-driving sex quite cruelly, she missed having a man's rigid flesh stretching her own. But she'd have missed not being with Piers more.

"You're the sweetest and kindest of girls," he said softly, his smile wry, "but you're a terrible liar! You're the sexiest creature I've ever met, my darling Hettie, and you need a damn good rogering! And often!"

"But—"

"No buts!" he said firmly, and even the small effort of raising his voice seemed to drain him. Sinking back against the pillows, he took her hand and clasped it with surprising force. "Will you trust me, Hett?" he asked. "Trust me and not ask questions?"

She nodded.

"I'm going to arrange something. Make something happen. I want you to accept it and enjoy it for my sake. Believe me, it'll make me as happy as it'll make you."

After that, she *did* question him, but he pleaded tiredness, smiled and went straight off to sleep.

The next night, Hettie had left him and returned to her own room, where she'd taken to sleeping so as not to disturb him with her tossing and turning. She'd just begun settling down to another sexless night, when the door opened and Starr stepped soundlessly into the room.

She opened her mouth to speak, then in her mind heard Piers' voice. "Trust me. No questions."

This—the arrival of his strong, virile servant—was Sir Piers Miller's "arrangement".

The dawning of this must have been clear on her face. Still without speaking, Starr walked over to the bed and looked down at her. His glacier blue eyes were calm, yet they were asking. She too had to agree. To want him...

It wasn't difficult. Though she'd been in love with Piers since they'd first met, she was red-blooded enough to appreciate the charms of other men.

And Starr had charms in abundance. He was tall and long-limbed, with broad shoulders and a slim tapered waist. His torso rippled with muscle and his whole body was in superb condition, but in no way heavy. His face was handsome and sculpted, his high cheekbones and hard jawline vaguely hawkish but strangely exciting. To round all this off he had the most piercing and unnaturally blue eyes Hettie had ever seen, and hair that was almost platinum blond. What she could see of it from his brutal, militaristic crew cut.

And when he slipped off the thin robe that was all that clothed him, she saw one of the most impressive cocks she'd ever had the luck to encounter! Thick, with defined veins and almost angry with life, it was frighteningly long and already erect as he lifted the single sheet and climbed into her bed beside her.

To her surprise, any guilt she might have felt ebbed as she moved into Starr's strong arms. The man would not have come here if it wasn't what Piers had wanted. And she realized—as she laid her fingers on the warm, velvet skin that sheathed Starr's mighty erection—that this was what she wanted too.

She knew nothing whatsoever of the inner life of her husband's enigmatic servant. She was even a little afraid and in awe of the cool, remote blond. But right now, in her lonely nocturnal frustration, she did want him. Furiously. Fabulously. Totally. Starr read her mind and slid his long fingers into her sex, stirring a heavy wetness there that shocked her. He'd only been in the room a couple of minutes and her pussy was running with slick moisture. She curled her hand around his cock and started edging him closer to the place that screamed for him. Starr responded by rubbing her clitoris.

And rubbing and rubbing and rubbing until she had her first quick, light orgasm. With a cry of surprise as much as pleasure, she let go her hold on his cock and squirmed like an eel beneath his touch. While her vagina still pulsed and fluttered, he pushed her gently onto her back, parted her legs and with no poking or probing, no help at all from his hand or hers, thrust into her right to the hilt.

"Oh God, I—" Whatever she might have said was crushed under Starr's kiss, and pounded out of her as he started fucking her fast and hard.

It was just what she needed. And probably, she acknowledged, half hysterical with sensation, exactly what Piers had ordered for her. Starr had always served the Millers faultlessly, and his performance in bed was no exception. This was the rough primitive sex that Hettie had missed so much. Even when he'd been able to make love, Piers had always been gentle and courtly.

But Starr was fucking her! Shagging her, powering into

her and giving her everything a strong, graceful lover could give her! As he thrust into her again and again, stretching her slippery sex in every direction, she screamed and groaned and shouted, hoping that Piers was awake and listening and aware of how much she appreciated what he'd sent to her.

Within minutes, she came again. And again. In this too Starr seemed superhuman. She knew he lifted weights, jogged and practiced a variety of martial arts. She ought to have known he'd be a sexual athlete par excellence too. He seemed inexhaustible, thrusting smoothly and deeply with no sign of either flagging or coming himself. It was Hettie, eventually, who had to sob, "Enough! Please… I…I'm going to pass out!"

Never in her short but enthusiastic sexual life had she come so much and so powerfully. But there was a limit even to ecstasy.

With one final manic lunge, Starr shot his scalding, creamy tribute deep inside her and the heat of it, the fine pulsing spurt of it against her spasming womb, brought a wave of pleasure so acute she really did start to pass out. Tears of relief and gratitude dried on her face as she slid slowly from consciousness. Her last awareness was Starr lifting himself neatly clear of her body.

Mister Perfect, precise as ever, was her final thought before oblivion.

And that was how it'd been throughout those final months with Piers.

By day she would spend her time with her increasingly feeble husband. Talking to him, reading to him, enjoying the benefits of his still-ready wit and his erudite comments on life, the universe and everything. He would inquire quite shamelessly about her sexual well-being and laugh at her blushes as she supplied the details he demanded. The raunchier her escapades, the better Piers liked it.

And her accounts *were* raunchy. Because by night she was getting better sex with just one man than she'd had with any of the lovers she'd had before her marriage.

Starr was skilled and inventive, just as much an artist in bed as he was a technician. The satisfaction, the orgasms he gave her at night were a soothing anodyne to the growing anguish of seeing a loved one die.

If she'd been asked to comment on such a relationship before she'd been in it, Hettie would have been horrified. Filled with disgust and revulsion. But as Piers slipped slowly but surely away from them, it seemed that the knowledge of his young wife's continuing sexual fulfillment was the one thing that lifted his spirits.

On that last morning, Piers had died in her arms—with Starr ever watchful in attendance—a final devilish smile on his lips as he'd listened to an explicit description of the previous night's pleasures.

Yes, Starr was the one who'd stood beside her as her husband had died, and the one who'd sustained her at his funeral. He was the one who'd supported her in every way. He was the one who'd run her household and maintained the pattern of her life while she'd fought to come to terms with her loss.

It was difficult to remember what she'd done with herself during the early months of her widowhood. But Starr had been the one constant reassuring presence, always there when she needed him.

And it was Starr's strong arms, beautiful golden-tanned

body, and virile, thrusting cock that had finally brought both her body and her heart back to life last night.

Mysterious Starr was both her servant and her lover, and now, revivified by the power of the sex that joined them, she was going to breach his wall of silence…even if it killed her!

Chapter Two

I must've been out of my mind to agree to this!
The next day, Hettie walked into the First Class Lounge at Heathrow to await the arrival of her mysterious visitor.

Almost before she'd framed the words in her mind, she was blushing. Hot blood rose in her face and throat, staining her ivory skin as erotic images formed.

Of course, she'd been out of her mind. She'd been floating in orgasmic euphoria when she'd said yes. She'd had Starr naked in her bed, and his fingers moving skillfully in the folds of her sex. Was it any wonder she hadn't been thinking too clearly?

Starr had been gone when she'd woken up, of course. He'd never once stayed the whole night while Piers had been alive, so she supposed it shouldn't have surprised her that he hadn't still been beside her this morning. Yet there'd been a clearly defined indentation where he'd lain, and when she'd rolled into it—breathing in his subtle spice and citrus cologne and the blood-stirring tangs of his sweat and his semen—she'd found that the pillow and the sheet were still warm.

Yes, he'd been close most of the night, and fucked her—repeatedly—with a healing tenderness and vigor. But as he'd handed her into the back of her limousine for their journey here to the airport, his strong golden face had been as still and unrevealing as ever. And there was nothing in his smooth, athletic body language to give any hint that he'd spent so many of the hours of darkness at work between her thighs.

Damn you, Starr! Confused feelings threatened to capsize her sense of sexual well-being. *You never acknowledge what we share! You never give a thing away! Doesn't it mean anything to you?*

Don't I mean anything to you?

Surely I must though, she thought. Nobody could make love with such power and tenderness and feel nothing. When she'd been in his arms last night, and he'd been inside her, she could have sworn she'd heard some inner voice of his, telling her his true feelings. Telling her wonders... If he was purely fucking her as a "service", that sense of contact wouldn't have been there, would it? Surely? And yet she had a disquieting feeling that it was going to be even harder than ever now to unravel the inner workings of her tall, blond lover's mind...and his heart.

This is such bad timing! Twisting the strap of her bag, she flopped down onto one of the lounge's luxurious deeply upholstered couches to wait for the arrival of the next flight from Milan. Even just from Renata's jumbled account last night, Hettie already felt a real sympathy for the lost and displaced Darryl, but to have him arrive now? When she already had enough on her plate trying to work out how to break through Starr's defenses?

Sighing, and still grappling with her confused thoughts, she smoothed her fingers nervously down the seam of her close-fitting black jeans, thinking of Renata's hastily scrawled fax that'd been waiting on the breakfast table this morning.

Hettie had been hoping for a day or two breathing space at least, but no, it seemed Darryl would be arriving this morning—on any one of three different flights!—and that he'd been given a photo of his hostess and would spot her at the airport himself!

Thanks, Ren. Thanks a bunch! Why the hell can't you embrace modern technology like the rest of us and email me *a photograph of* him? *It isn't too much to ask.* But Ren was probably back in bed with the obnoxious-sounding Fausto by now, having blissfully cast off all responsibility for her confused charge.

Shifting uncomfortably in her seat, Hettie tried to discreetly adjust her clothing. Last night's athleticism, and Starr's size and strength, had taken a toll on the most intimate areas of her anatomy. Her pussy felt delicately inflamed, and even though her black silk bra was almost weightless, it still chafed against her swollen, well-mouthed nipples. And the trouble with these discomforts was that they induced a vicious circle. The more she'd been petted and fondled and stroked, the more sensitive her erogenous zones became. And the more sensitive they were, the more easily they became aroused. Which meant she was on fire to be caressed again. Right here in this most public of public places! Trying to ignore the fact that she desperately wanted to be back in Starr's arms, with his firm penis moving inside her, she set her mind to the imminent arrival.

I suppose he'll be a bit of a nerd.

Years spent scrabbling around antiquities with an eccentric archaeologist wasn't likely to produce poise, confidence and social self-awareness. But still, she'd been bookish herself in her youth, and there was nothing wrong with being a geek.

Nevertheless, Hettie felt uneasy as she looked around the discreetly busy lounge.

And I'm supposed to teach the poor devil about sex? I think not, Ren. I think not...

But as she scanned the occupant of the couch next to hers, her sensual awareness piqued, despite everything.

I wouldn't mind teaching him *a thing or two!* she thought, feeling profoundly ashamed that she could think lustful thoughts about another man while she was still in such an emotional turmoil over Starr. Even so, she blushed again as her sensitized body responded automatically to the figure asleep a few feet away, her bruised nipples puckering a little and her soft sexual furrow growing decidedly moist.

He was a truly remarkable-looking male.

"Sleeping beauty" was youngish, Latinate and angelically handsome. His impossibly long legs were encased in form-fitting designer denim, and a cloudlike white linen shirt was the most perfect foil for his toffee-colored Mediterranean complexion. Tousled hair—black as pitch and nearly as long as her own—tumbled to his lean shoulders, and she could swear she'd never seen a pair of thicker or more luscious eyelashes or a mouth that so plainly begged for kisses.

Dear God, what kind of fickle disgusting slut am I?

Almost as if it her libido had absolutely nothing to do with her finer feelings, Hettie felt her pussy quicken and more wetness pool between her legs. But the man *was* remarkable. It wasn't enough that he'd got a face straight out of a Renaissance fresco, he'd also got a classical body. The blue denim crotch of his jeans was breathtakingly stretched and bulging.

Oh my, it's indecent being that size in jeans so tight!

Suddenly, Hettie found herself grinning, despite her confusion. Her emotions were all over the map right now, but there was a real joy in feeling alive and horny again. She'd never know what this glorious stranger was like as a lover, but surely there was no real sin in a bit of harmless fantasizing? And wouldn't Starr himself eventually reap the benefits? When she channeled her reborn needs in his direction?

One excuse is as good as another, the wry voice of honesty told her mockingly.

For a moment, she entertained a vivid fantasy of Starr satisfying her with his hard-thrusting cock while this delicious but unknown man ran his hands over her body. Would they both go for it? She knew that Starr would do whatever she requested of him, and the guy beside her was probably frisky enough to be ready for anything.

She was still smiling, and still inwardly quivering, when the man's thick eyelashes fluttered open and revealed the deepest chocolate-brown eyes she'd ever seen. Eyes that first clouded and looked perplexed, then widened and lit with a wild bright light of relief.

He recognizes me! Then it dawned on her. *Omigod, this's Darryl!*

Confused, she sprang to her feet. Just as the beautiful man did the same, then stepped towards her, tall and lithe, and with his amazing face wreathed in an almost ecstatic smile.

"Lady Henrietta! I'm so glad you're here! I thought I was going to miss you!"

"Darryl?"

"Oh yes... Yes, I'm Darryl." The voice was soft and light, and the accent as sexy as the face and body that went with it. "I'm sorry. I got my flights mixed up. I'm early." He held out a long, skinny-fingered hand, and without hesitation, Hettie let her own be grasped.

Confusing heat enveloped her and she shuddered. Quite taken aback, she just stood there, trying to accept that this gorgeous, stylishly dressed demigod was the very same naïve innocent she'd come here to meet.

This was the archeologist with no memory?

Hettie felt strangely shaky. She'd rarely felt this affected by a man on first meeting him. The exceptions were when she'd met Piers, so suave, mature and sophisticated—and ended up in his bed the very same evening. And almost at the same time, when she'd met her new lover's enigmatic blond servant, the same man who'd just last night filled her yearning sex with his flesh, and her heart with muddled emotions.

Thinking of Starr now reminded her that he was waiting for them with the car. She felt a rush of guilt at feeling so turned on by Darryl.

"Do you have luggage or anything?" she asked. He still appeared tired, but nevertheless his composure was rock-solid. For an amnesiac who had just been tossed out onto the street by his only remaining relative, his self-possession was remarkable.

"Yes. Here," he said, gesturing to a neat stack of belongings. One elegant Gucci suitcase, a matching flight bag and a butter-soft black leather jacket draped across the top of the two.

"Okay. Pass me the bag. We can manage these between us. No use hanging about here for porterage when we've a car waiting to take us home."

Without actually refusing her help, Darryl whisked up all his items of luggage, smiled impishly like a hypersexed angel then fell into step beside her as they left the lounge on their way to find Starr and the limousine.

Hettie's very personal assistant was predictably unfazed

by the unexpected glamour of Darryl di Angeli. She watched, vaguely aware that her mouth had fallen open, as the two men stowed the bags away in the boot of the limo and chatted about Darryl's flight and his sketchy knowledge of England.

Hettie could hardly believe the mad, sexy thoughts that passed through her mind, at the sight of the two of them. Piers' fond, indulgent laughter echoed in her ears as she stood and stared at possibly the two most desirable men in all of greater London talking easily together as if they'd known each other ages. And as first Starr helped her into the car, then Darryl slid gracefully onto the back seat beside her, she reflected that she couldn't have found two more diametrically different examples of male pulchritude if she'd gone out and actively looked for them.

Starr, so cool and hard, so strong and remorselessly knowing. And now Darryl, with his skinny long-limbed beauty, his huge, dark, lost eyes and his peculiar combination of naïveté and confidence. The only common factor they shared was a solid male bulge in their jeans.

As Starr eased the car smoothly away from the curb, Hettie wondered how on earth to open a conversation with the man beside her. What did one say to someone who'd lost his or her memory? Once again she was struck by the enormity of what she'd agreed to do.

Here was someone who'd lost both the person who'd been closest to him in all the world, and any recollection of what he'd done with his life to date. Not to mention the more intimate memory loss that Renata had not too subtly hinted at. Darryl's apparent inability to remember whether he'd ever had sex or not.

Panicking, she plunged in with the first thing that came into her head, "That's a very nice shirt, Darryl. Did you get it in Milan?"

It was banal. Wooden. But her companion turned to her, smiled cheerfully and touched his long brown fingers to the immaculate white fabric.

"Why yes," he said, his light, deliciously Latin voice playing tunes on her trembling nerves. "I chose it myself. I chose all my new clothes myself. Do you like it?"

"You've been *shopping*?" How bizarre! If he'd lived a life of semi-academic seclusion, and just suffered a tragic blow, fashion ought to have been an unknown quantity to him. But it seemed that he'd instinctively chosen things that suited his looks. Italian style was obviously bred into the bone.

"Yes, it was fun," Darryl answered lightly, "I found some magazines belonging to F—" he faltered then, his smooth features crumpling for just a second. "To Cousin Renata's friend. I saw beautiful clothes on every page, so when they arranged a credit card for me, I just wandered around the shops until I saw similar things, then I went in and bought them."

"You went shopping on your own?" What on earth was wrong with Ren? Leaving someone who'd lost their memory and was fresh out of hospital entirely to their own devices in a big cosmopolitan city.

"I think Cousin Renata would've liked to have gone with me, but—" He paused, delicately, and Hettie understood the uncomfortable situation that must've prevailed at Palazzo di Angeli. And what a hideous, selfish and unfeeling man Renata had got herself hooked up with.

"Was this Fausto guy hostile towards you?" she asked sharply, studying the perfect, Renaissance face of the man beside her.

"I think…I think he felt threatened by me," Darryl answered, sounding remarkably perceptive. "I was a challenge to his supremacy. And he was jealous when Renata tried to be nice to me."

Hettie's jaw dropped. Lord, he was impressive! She'd expected Darryl to be awkward, geeky and not particularly sure of himself, but he was nothing of the sort! The quiet wisdom of his answer confounded all her preconceptions. If he could so accurately assess the power balance of his cousin's shaky relationships, he could well be far less naïve— and in a lot more ways!—than Hettie had been led to believe.

Sneaking a glance sideways, she caught him in the midst of a huge but politely smothered yawn.

"*Mi scusi!*" he said softly, rocking Hettie's defenses with a smile of heartbreaking sweetness, "I haven't been sleeping too well since… Since…" The smile was replaced by a frown which in its own way was just a sexy. "Since everything."

Hettie felt a great wave of tenderness rush through her, something vaguely maternal, but in other ways not motherly at all. She imagined hugging him and comforting, but at the same time wondered what it would be like to see him without his clothes, and to caress his body and stroke his eager cock to hardness.

Dear God!

The sensation had been so intense and physical that she gasped, and her eyes flew to the back of Starr's blond head, wondering if he could sense her shameless imaginings. When her eyes flicked back to Darryl, he was frowning again, his eyes grown dark with remorse.

"I'm sorry," he apologized again, "I forgot… My condolences on the death of your husband."

He'd misinterpreted her response, of course. She was fantasizing about sex in a way her late husband would have heartily approved of. But Darryl obviously felt guilty for reminding of her loss by mentioning his own. What a mess!

"Darryl," she said quietly, turning to face him and trying

to ignore a sudden mad urge to kiss him, "Don't worry about me. I was sad for my husband but I'm coming to terms with his death now." She couldn't help but flick her eyes towards Starr's broad back again, separated from them by the glass partition as he steered the car skillfully into a stream of traffic. "And I'd like to help you."

Impulsively she reached for his hand, then almost flinched at the sensual heat of his skin. "I'm here for you, Darryl, however you need me." This was insanely rash, but she still said it, "You only have to ask... But there's no pressure. You don't have to do anything but relax. Take it easy." What was she saying? Maybe she should back off a bit? "In fact, if you feel tired now, you could have a nap in the car. It's quite a drive back into town in this traffic."

The look in Darryl's eyes was enigmatic. There in those brown depths was an unexpected quality of knowingness that was one of the sexiest things Hettie had ever seen, yet his verbal answer was strangely mild and noncommittal.

"Thank you. You're very kind. I do feel tired. But I'll try not to fall asleep. It'd be a bit rude, wouldn't it? When we've only just met."

Words seemed superfluous, and although they did chat for a few minutes about their destination and other neutral topics, a companionable silence soon descended over them.

Companionable, but for Hettie, not exactly comfortable. As Darryl's sooty eyelashes drifted down again, and he did indeed fall asleep, she realized he was still holding her hand. She felt every sense in her body come to sudden demanding life. The warm fingers that curved around hers seemed to burn her trembling skin.

Unthinkable as it was, after barely an hour of knowing him, she found herself desiring this beautiful man. A wave of guilt tore through her, but she couldn't seem to prevent her mind and her imagination from running wild!

It was easy to imagine Darryl nude. His body would be the same sleek toffee tan as his face and the long, sensual hand that still rested in hers. He'd be lean, obviously, and she pictured his chest silky and hairless and his groin heavily furred with deepest black. His sex—oh boy!—would be generous, jutting imperiously from his loins. She saw him now, in her mind's eye, superbly erect, his stiff shaft rearing up in tribute to her beauty, the tip red and hugely distended, the slit open and weeping a stream of clear juice.

Trying to breathe slowly and lightly, so as not to disturb him, she settled back into the seat, closed her own eyes and tried to find some inner calm. Some control over the images that clamored in her mind.

This is insane! I'm not sex maniac! Not everything has to be erotic!

But the images were impossible to quell, and she felt again that strange sensation of her sex drive cutting loose from her emotions.

With a soundless sigh, she let the fantasy pour right over her. Shifting her legs, she surreptitiously adjusted her bottom so that the hard-stitched seam of her jeans went deep into the cleft of her sex. When she edged an inch or two closer to the edge of the seat, the slack was taken up and the stiff unyielding ridge pressed hard against the swollen bud of her clitoris. All she needed to do now was wriggle, and she could masturbate without even using her fingers. Squirming discreetly, she tried to summon Darryl's naked but imaginary body to the center stage of her mind.

But he was gone.

She blinked her eyes open, and knew the cause. It was directly in front of her. In the form of a strongly shaped male skull and dizzyingly blond hair, shaven short.

Her fantasy reassembled itself, and even though the beautiful Darryl stood on the sidelines, naked and touching himself, it was Starr lying on her bed. Starr, bare, erect and inviting.

Hettie stood beside him, her thin lace slip accentuating her body and its aroused state rather than concealing it. Her dark, swollen nipples were clearly visible, and likewise the tantalizing shadow of her lush pubic curls. As she got onto the bed, kneeling beside him, his electric blue eyes flared with lust, and that mighty cock she knew so well trembled in tribute. Acknowledging his salute, she took his strong, capable hand in hers and guided his fingers beneath the skimpy slip and straight into the wet fevered heat of her pussy.

"Stroke me, Starr," she whispered, commanding softly, "Touch me. Make me come." Her body spoke too, reinforcing her words as she rocked her aching clit on him, making a firm pleasure-giving fulcrum out of the side of his outstretched hand. Using her mind-pictures shamelessly, she worked her loins to and fro, her fantasy self jiggling the tiny nub of her clitoris and laughing in exultation as her moisture welled from within her and trickled out over the whole of Starr's hand and wrist.

Adjusting herself forward she pressed her bare thigh against the slick shaft of his cock, then reached up to flip down the spaghetti straps of her slip and make her swollen breasts bare. Taking them one in each hand she began to squeeze and knead in time to the rhythm of her jerking hips. She was putting on a show for him. Just for him. Darryl had vanished. Her lewd performance was purely for the beautiful man on the bed. To pleasure him. To honor him. To breach the stern defenses he'd built around a generous, loving heart.

Enflamed by emotion as well as by lust, she saw her

servant-lover catch the same fire. Thrashing on the bed, he moved his body around with a frenzy that was as far away from his usual iron control as night was from day. His eyes locked with hers and he worked his lean hips and rubbed his sticky shaft against her. Then finally—with a resigned groan of surrender—he took his flesh in his own fingers and began to jerk himself in frantic time to Hettie's own rhythm.

Within a few moments he sobbed, arced up from the sheets and pure white semen pulsed out onto Hettie's bare thigh. Thick heavy spurts of it anointed her. Its heat, and the rich, pungent aroma of it as it trickled across her skin, were too much for the hunger of her senses. She gave a great animal-like cry, pumped her hips in a blur then came hard and fast and wet against his hand.

As orgasm consumed her, both in dream and reality, Hettie's eyes flew open, and she turned—in bemused and mortified embarrassment—to meet Darryl's calm, fascinated and utterly level stare.

Her face pink, Hettie struggled to find something to say. She experienced a huge rush of relief when her traveling companion suddenly turned and pointed out of the car window.

"Is this your house?" His soft voice gave no hint that he'd just watched her come. She could only nod, befuddled that the journey was already over and they were stationary in front of 17 Pengilley Gardens, the large London house that Piers had left her. Still stunned from her climax, and from knowing Darryl had seen and understood what'd happened, she felt incapable of coordinating or speaking. She could only thank her lucky stars—or more properly Starr—when the tall blond opened the car door and helped her out onto the pavement. She'd never leaned harder on his arm, nor felt more confused by her feelings.

"Are you all right, ma'am?" he inquired politely.

"Yes, I'm—"

No, she wasn't. When she tried to walk, she felt dizzy and swayed, and within seconds there were *two* strong men holding her up.

Like some kind of sprite, Darryl had darted around from the other side of the car, and was vying with Starr for the task of supporting the swooning damsel. If she hadn't felt so flustered, Hettie would have laughed. Two knights for one fair lady, not a bad ratio. Not bad at all.

This thought revived her, but as she mounted the shallow steps—with her honor guard still at her side—and the black-painted front door swung open, Hettie knew she needed time to think. This was all too much for her, not what she'd expected, and she needed time to organize her thoughts and understand her own emotions and desires.

Darryl was a beautiful man and sexually desirable, not just an unwanted houseguest to be coped with. And yet even when she'd found herself fantasizing about him, the cool image of Starr had effortlessly hijacked the waking dream.

He was taking her over, controlling her. And yet still he maintained his emotional distance.

With perfect, impeccable decorum, he suggested, "Perhaps you'd better lie down for a while, milady?" He let go of her arm but fixed her with his steely blue gaze. "I'll show Darryl his room and arrange for his things to be unpacked." He turned to Darryl, "And if you're hungry, Mrs. Phillips, our housekeeper, will make you a meal."

"No! I'm the hostess. I should be looking after Darryl!"

Hettie was speared by guilt. Darryl was a stranger in a strange land and she couldn't just turn him over to someone else straight away. No matter how embarrassed she was or how kind and welcoming Mrs. Phillips was.

"Thanks, Lady Henrietta…Starr… But it's all right." Darryl looked from Hettie to Starr, his smooth, face as calm as if he knew everything about their bizarre arrangement and found it unsurprising. "Please don't go to any trouble for me. If it's okay with you, I'd like to lie down for a while myself. I didn't sleep much last night."

"Me neither," said Hettie, then blushed furiously remembering the reason for her insomnia. Her eyes flicked automatically from man to man, checking for reaction as she quivered like a fawn in the curiously charged atmosphere around them.

Starr's face was a handsome, unrevealing mask as usual, but Darryl smiled, his eyes filled with that curious awareness again. He knew why she hadn't slept, and it was a subject of intense interest to him. His eyes flicked in Starr's direction for half a second, and it was all Hettie could do not to gasp aloud.

He knows, the bastard! He knows! she thought, when she was safe in the privacy of her room and Darryl was in the kind but fussy hands of Mrs. Phillips, the cook and housekeeper, who was Starr's opposite number and performed all the household duties that he didn't. Starr himself, faultlessly efficient as ever, was busy with the luggage and the car, and Hettie was glad he was out of the way too. She'd sensed him watching her closely in those last few moments with Darryl, as if monitoring her responses, ticking off the telltale signs of her arousal, and logging the progress of this unexpected new dynamic.

"Why the hell can't you be jealous?" she demanded of him

in his absence, darting around her room, unable to settle in one place for a second. She wished Starr were with her right now so she could pound her fists against that smooth, golden chest of his in the vain hope that she might force some kind of revelation out of him. Some kind of acknowledgement.

If you'd just say something, Starr, just give me some kind of sign, I'd send Darryl away this instant. Find someone else to take him in, take care of him...and bloody well educate him!

Just say something, you blond devil, say something!

Confused, she threw herself facedown on the bed, trying desperately to calm her whirling thoughts and her surging hormones.

Last night, on this very same bed, she'd been opened and taken by Starr. Had more sex in a few hours than some women had in a month. But right now, on these fresh crisp sheets and the pristine pink bedspread, she was ready to be taken again. At least that way she and Starr were close, exquisitely joined and intimate, and his body said everything his lack of words didn't.

The vision from the car returned again. Herself with her tall, ice god of a servant whose long cock and skillful fingers could thrill her to madness. And the watchful visitor from Italy observing them.

Moving uneasily, she rubbed her tingling breasts against the counterpane and tried to remember if she'd ever felt like this while Piers was alive. They'd had some wonderful times, but surely she'd never felt as hungry and as sluttish as she did now?

Maybe I should masturbate? Clear my mind of it all with one huge orgasm. She lifted her hips from the bed, and was just sliding her fingers beneath her, when there was a firm, sharp, tellingly familiar knock at the door.

"Come in, Starr," she called out, dropping down again

and quickly pulling her hand out.

"Are you all right, milady?" he asked quietly from the side of the bed. His steps had been so quick and light that she'd barely heard him approach.

"Yes, I'm fine, thanks, Starr," she lied, knowing he knew it was a lie. "I'm just a bit tense." Closing her eyes, she lay still, half wanting him to leave her alone with her problem, half wanting him to stay and deal with it.

He stayed.

"A neck massage might do the trick, ma'am."

What trick?

Starr knelt on the bed beside her, his black-clad knee brushing the side of her breast. Without being asked she opened the top of her blouse and eased it awkwardly off her shoulders. She felt him lift her thick hair to one side and spread it over the pillow.

"Just relax," he whispered, but she shuddered violently when he slid her bra straps down her arms. He'd hardly uncovered any of her, really, yet she felt as if he'd bared her sex and stroked it. She moaned aloud when his fingers went cleverly to work.

She'd no idea if Starr had any formal training as a masseur, but he was a master and an artist with his thumbs. Light as a feather at her hairline and down her spine, but firm and almost brutal as he dug into the taut knotted muscles of her upper back. Looming over her, he leaned his strong frame determinedly into each and every stroke, and as one tension drained away, Hettie felt another more crucial one flood in.

Shifting his weight for purchase, Starr threw a long leg across her, and enclosed both her thighs between his. Hettie quivered beneath his gliding hands. His sex was barely an inch above hers and she couldn't help imagining him hard. Hard as he'd been last night, inside her. Hard as she was soft and liquid.

"Relax, ma'am," he murmured again, his big hands working their way across her shoulders, then smoothing down the backs of her arms to her fisted hands bunching against the bed. "Relax, ma'am, go loose."

"I can't," she whimpered, her crotch a mass of fire as her bottom wafted upward in search of him. Shimmying with a hunger that never really seemed to go away, but just lie quiescent from time to time.

Starr was erect now, and Hettie rubbed against his hardness with her softness. She felt ashamed of her own crude invitation, yet in an odd way reveled in it. Starr's hands left hers, then traveled back up her arms and slid beneath her body, cupping her still-covered breasts without a word of warning or enquiry. In silence, he continued his treatment, caressing her swollen nipples with all the clinical methodism he'd used on her neck and her shoulders. His weight shifted and his center of gravity dropped slightly, and through several layers of clothing, Hettie felt his cock nudge her ass.

For several long minutes, he rubbed his hardness slowly against her, riding the groove of her bottom with the same slow rhythm he was using on her breasts.

Is he doing this for himself?

Or was it solely a service to her? Through jeans and underclothes she could feel his bulge caressing her anus. Hot streaks of pleasure seemed to pulse from the point of contact and shoot straight to all the rest of her that wanted him. Her sensitized breasts throbbed in his grip, her clitoris ached, her pussy felt empty and needy and longing for the solace of his cock.

"Starr, please… Oh please, for God's sake!" she croaked, abandoning every shred of her pride.

As the last word still hung in the air, the pressure was lifted away from her bottom and she felt Starr rearranging their bodies. He moved with uncanny lightness for one so large and muscular, but within seconds he was further back somehow, between her knees instead of enclosing hers in his.

Mute and pliant, she felt his hands on her hips, lifting her pelvis until she was on all fours, her hips tilted. Then his fingers swooped under her, finding the fastening of her jeans and quickly and deftly uncovering her. In seconds she had the black denim cloth bunched awkwardly at her knees and only a pair of tiny black panties to shield her—a skimpy nonsense of satin and lace that'd slipped into the groove of her bottom.

The pants themselves made her feel sleazy, less covered somehow than she would have been without them. They were damp at the crotch, and she knew Starr would be able to see it. See juiciness and see her lust. He'd know that to create so large a stain she must have been creaming and yearning for hours, thinking both of him, and of her angelic new houseguest.

For a split second, Hettie imagined it was Darryl kneeling behind her while Starr watched. Darryl staring at her white flesh and her wet black pants. Darryl, revealed and rampant, poised to fuck her. She pictured Starr's solemn face suddenly contorting with pure male jealousy. And possessiveness. In her fantasy, he pushed the younger man aside, banishing him as he, Starr, claimed his woman.

And then it was just Starr, the perfect lover offering everything she needed and perhaps ever would need. Cool, accomplished Starr, sliding down his zipper, easing out his thick red penis then dragging its oozing tip against the surface of her inner thigh.

Is he going to take me with my pants on? Would he push

the gusset out of the way, and push in beside it, caressing his own length with the satin? Her sex quivered as if inviting him to do it like that, and her bottom jutted back at him of its own accord.

Please take me! her body screamed silently as she marveled at the inner pictures. Her black-clad form, waiting and utterly lewd. Her rounded white ass, with cheeks exposed but bisected by a thin swath of silk.

At the very last second she felt him pause, hover, then catch the elastic of her panties and push them down her thighs. With everything bunched at her knees, his access was limited. It felt gloriously primal and exciting. So intense that there was no time for niceties or comfort. Her pussy was swimming with silky, welcoming moisture as he nudged at her entrance, but hampered as she was, her legs couldn't properly open and he had to reach down and peel back her labia to admit him.

She moaned as his fingers explored her sex, opening her up, readying her. "Fuck me!" she exhorted him, jamming herself backwards against him, desperate to join with him. "Fuck me, Starr! Oh dear heaven, I want you inside me! Now!" she shouted, appalled at how wanton she sounded, but loving that he could make her that way.

Starr's cock probed but didn't enter.

He was teasing her, holding back, but Hettie was delirious for him. With a strangled cry, she slammed herself backwards, frantic for their bodies to become one.

There was a shockingly wet sound of flesh sliding against fluid and then he was fully and deeply inside her, thrown across her back like a cloak of loving heat while his stiff penis throbbed in her channel. He was bearing his weight on one hand, but she felt the other curl around her thigh, his fingers digging in as he fought for maximum leverage.

Thrusting steadily, he went right to the core of her, beating on her clitoris from within as he fucked her with exactly the primitive intensity she needed. Hettie buried her face in the pillow, stifling her cries of animal pleasure, her heart full of grateful wonder that he could read her desires so perfectly.

"Touch yourself, Hettie," he ordered with a shocking, unfamiliar raggedness. Her given name was harsh in her ear as he stroked relentlessly into her, all his quiet-spoken courtesy lost in the ferment of sex. "Do it! Stroke yourself! Make yourself come!"

Falling forward, she obeyed him, forcing her hand between the bed and her body. Scrabbling in the heat and wetness between her shaking thighs, she sought out that tiny bundle of screaming, strung-out nerves, that pure white point of ultimate sensation.

And when she found it, it was she who cried raggedly. The rush of her orgasm made her thrash and buck beneath him as finally his choking cry of release graced her ears.

"My lady! Oh, my lady!" he sobbed as he came inside her, his essence bathing her womb as surely as his heartfelt words fed her soul.

Chapter Three

Are they doing it now?
Darryl looked down at the book on his lap, then upward in the general direction of Lady Henrietta's bedroom, trying to imagine a real scene, and real, beautiful bodies, rather than just a black-and-white photograph.

Well, if they weren't making love now, there was no doubt they'd done it earlier, because he'd heard them. Heard the harsh impassioned cries that were so like the noises he'd heard at Palazzo di Angeli when his cousin and Fausto had excused themselves and disappeared for hours on end. He'd known without being told that what he'd been hearing were the noises of sex. An activity that seemed to haunt his mind and his body even though he couldn't seem to summon any memories of actually engaging in it himself.

Why can't I remember having sex? He frowned at the illustration he'd been studying. Per Dio, *it's just not possible I could forget doing* that!

When Darryl had woken up in a clean white Milan hospital room, his greatest feeling had been loss. Pure, aching loss. Loss of people and loss of places. Loss of the whole of his life somehow.

He knew who he was. He knew his thoughts, his personality and his likes and dislikes. But it was the world around him that he'd forgotten. It'd disappeared, leaving only the vaguest fragments to frustrate him. Brief flashes, of which he couldn't make sense and which gave him headaches when he tried to force them into focus. In the end he'd given up trying to remember and just taken the doctor's advice. Which had been to relax and let his brain take its own time to heal and yield up the lost memories.

It was a hard thing to cope with, yet in spite of everything there had been gains as well as losses. The thing he'd taken to calling his "awareness".

Darryl had a new power, an ability he was certain he hadn't had before. Even if he had no way of knowing.

It wasn't exactly mind reading or ESP. It wasn't as clear-cut as that. What it felt like was hard to put into words. The only comparison was a set of mental cat's whiskers that were sensitive to currents of emotion. To feelings and moods. And especially sex.

Which was ironic, given his lack of sexual memories and his total inability to remember whether he'd ever made love to a woman!

Since his accident he'd certainly wanted to fuck. Often and achingly so.

The first time had been in the clinic itself with the kind, dark-haired nurse. He'd got stiff while she was tending to him. She hadn't been pretty—in fact she'd been fat and homely—but her breasts had been round and soft as pillows and as she'd leant across him, his penis had risen up and pointed at them in tribute. The sight of that had made her eyes sparkle, and she'd told him "not to worry, it was only natural" and then taken him firmly in her gentle hands and rubbed him until he'd sobbed out his release.

After that she'd masturbated him every day, sometimes more than once, and evaded him cleverly when he'd tried to caress her in return. "You'll soon have women falling over themselves for you, *ragazzo*," she'd told him cheerfully. "And with a face and body like yours, it'll be the beauties that want you. Plain old things like me won't get a look in."

And Renata, his adopted cousin, *was* a beauty! Darryl couldn't remember having sex, but he did know what it was and he'd wanted it immediately when he'd seen Renata. His new awareness had told him that she returned the feeling but it'd also told him she was almost as confused and scared as he was. At the Palazzo di Angeli, the ancestral residence of his adoptive family, he'd found out the reason. Fausto, who'd hated him on sight and didn't even seem to like Renata all that much. The two of them had frequent and very noisy bouts of lovemaking that drove Darryl's fingers irresistibly to his crotch. But even though he was concerned for Renata and hated leaving her, he'd also been relieved when she'd haltingly told him it'd be better if he were to live somewhere else for a while.

Which had led him here, to 17 Pengilley Gardens, London, England, the home of Lady Henrietta Miller, Renata's recently bereaved and astoundingly beautiful English friend. Another rare and sensual woman who already had a lover.

Things were different in this house though. He could sense it. There were currents of sadness and loss from the death of the late Sir Piers, but on the whole Darryl already felt much more relaxed than he had at the palazzo.

What'd happened in the car with Lady Henrietta—or Hettie as she insisted he call her—had made his head spin and his groin feel like bursting, but afterward he'd sensed no animosity in her. Quite the contrary. Hettie was confused like her friend Renata, but she also found him attractive.

She'd suffered a devastating bereavement but at heart she was fighting her grief with a vibrancy and love of life that fired Darryl's blood and made him hopeful for his own future happiness.

And Lady Hettie's lover was far less hostile than Fausto.

It was obvious that *Signor* Starr and Hettie fucked. Darryl had felt the vibes immediately, the palpable erotic current that arced between the lady and her servant even when they were yards apart. Darryl's heart had at sunk at first, expecting polite animosity from the tall blond, but after a few moments of chatting with Starr he realized his fears were unfounded. True, the man was somewhat cool and remote, but that seemed to be his nature rather than anything specifically directed at Darryl. Starr seemed to adhere to a very old-fashioned standard of discreet, unobtrusive service in public. It was only in private that Darryl suspected that things were very, very different.

The book he was studying was not one of the ones Mrs. Phillips had pointed him to when he'd first come down to the library.

When he'd woken up after a long refreshing sleep he'd dressed and wandered downstairs. The brisk but kindly housekeeper had provided him with tea and a snack and then had shown him briefly around the house. She hadn't mentioned the whereabouts of Hettie and Starr, and Darryl hadn't asked.

After his tour, Mrs. P had settled him in the cozy wood-paneled library and shown him roughly how the vast assembly of books was arranged. She'd pointed out history, geography and various classics. She'd also shown him Hettie's selection of contemporary novels, science fiction and thrillers. What she hadn't shown him, but what he'd found for himself was what seemed to be an extensive collection of extremely explicit erotica. The book he'd finally chosen was a superb photographic anthology bound in white leather. The theme was sexual intercourse.

He flicked the pages slowly, frowning at his frustrating lack of knowledge yet at the same simmering with excitement. The broad idea of fucking was familiar to him, it was coded into the genes and so basic to life that instruction was unnecessary. But it was the refinements that Darryl was curious about. Where did women like to be touched? What gave them pleasure? How could he make it better for a woman without exciting himself so much that he came immediately?

Studying a picture of a man holding a woman's breasts, he could see that she was enjoying the sensations. Her face was distorted and her teeth bared, but he could tell it was pleasure she was feeling not pain. He imagined what Hettie's breasts might look like with a man's hands upon them. The image of her was clear and beautiful, but in his imagination, all he saw was her, not the man.

Hettie had gorgeous breasts. They were just the right size. When he'd seen her nipples harden in the car, his cock had stiffened in his jeans. And just thinking about them now had the very same effect. He could feel—and see—his erection pushing up against the zipper and bulging inside the blue denim. He laid his hand lightly on the hot swollen place and with the other hand flipped over a page.

It was a close-up, done in black and white but he could imagine the colors. A man was caught just in the very moment of pushing his cock into a woman's sex. There were no faces or limbs, just the shot of the nested genitals and his finger touching her a little way above the penetration. The tip of his finger itself was pressed amongst the folds, resting on a tiny budlike structure. The clitoris. That was it! *Dio*, there was so much to remember... So much that he was sure he must have once known.

The man was in her. His cock was in her sex. Her pussy. And he was touching her clitoris.

Pressing harder on his cock, he imagined that the sex in the picture was Hettie's and that it was his finger dabbling in her wetness. Her pussy was pink, beautifully soft and wet, and she felt much better around him than his own hand ever could. Although even that felt pretty good at times.

The temptation to unzip himself now was almost unbearable, but there were people about the house who might come in and catch him exposed. The idea of Hettie seeing his cock made the organ itself throb dangerously. But he certainly didn't want Starr or Mrs. Phillips to walk in and catch him masturbating. Perhaps he could take the book to his room later? Look at it in a safe place and caress himself in comfort?

The next photograph had some similarities to the previous one. It was a close-up shot of a woman's sex, but this time there was no cock and no finger. A pointed tongue, either a man or a woman's, was licking at the swollen glistening flesh.

It was too much. Moaning, Darryl rubbed furiously at his cock through his jeans and imagined the taste of Hettie on his tongue. He couldn't believe that she wouldn't be delicious!

And the texture... In his imagination she was soft and yielding. And she cried out as he'd heard her this afternoon. Moisture flowed from her as sensation took her. A sensation that must be huge and sublimely beautiful if it in any way resembled *his* feelings when *he* came. If it was anything like the way he felt now, as he orgasmed helplessly and his semen pulsed out into his briefs while he threw his head back and groaned with pleasure.

"Darryl?"

Darryl heard the word quite clearly through the bliss of his climax. It was so distinct that he suddenly realized that it wasn't actually part of his fantasy. Looking up, blinking, he saw a figure standing near the doorway.

Lady Henrietta Miller, clad in a thin, floating, black silk evening dress. Her eyes were round and bright and a smile played around her soft, red mouth.

⁂

It was one of the most beautiful sights she'd ever seen, and even though Darryl was fully and modestly clothed it was supremely and breath-catchingly erotic.

Hettie had seen men touch themselves before. Piers had never been ashamed to masturbate for her, nor she for him, and she adored the sight of Starr casually fondling himself in preparation for a second bout of lovemaking.

But this was different. So pure, so unconscious, so uninhibited. A heavenly tableau... Darryl's hand was a blur at his crotch, his strong throat was arched and vulnerable and his smooth angelic face distorted as the supreme moment splintered his senses. It was everything she might have imagined of him and yet more, despite his lack of nudity.

As the crisis left him, she watched his slim hips drop back into the chair and his face and body relax.

Touché! You've watched me and now I've watched you. She almost spoke the words aloud, but before she could his eyes flicked open and she found herself smiling.

"I'm sorry. I disturbed you," she said, at a loss for anything else. As she watched, he shifted slightly in the great leather wing chair and her own sex shivered at the thought of how sticky and tingling his must be.

"It's perhaps as well," he replied, his voice astoundingly even as he closed his book, put it aside and rose politely to his feet. Hettie felt awed by him, taken aback that he could still be so self-possessed at a moment when another man might be tongue-tied and blushing with embarrassment. She felt herself blushing instead, her mind filling with images that were probably just as sexy as the ones to which Darryl had been masturbating.

Even when he wasn't coming, her handsome houseguest looked a picture. He'd obviously showered and changed, because his coal black hair had a soft damp sheen to it and his skin looked deliciously fresh. His form-fitting jeans were the same ones he'd arrived in, or some very similar, but he'd put on a clean shirt to come down to dinner. Another silk one, but this time short sleeved in a shade of palest lemon. The misty color was a perfect foil for the drama of his unbound hair and the rich butterscotch-brown of his skin and Hettie couldn't imagine any model in any magazine looking sexier.

"What's your book?" she inquired, trying hard not to sound squeaky and self-conscious. As she sat down in the chair next to Darryl's, he flopped down beside her and handed her the book.

Images d'Amour was a gorgeous volume. With an art degree and several years spent working in galleries before her marriage, Hettie could appreciate the work aesthetically as well as sexually. Perfectly shot photographs of couples making love were presented starkly with no superfluous text. It was no wonder that Darryl had become aroused. The photos got to Hettie too, every time she looked at them.

"It excited me," he said as she flicked the pages, his tone quite casual as if masturbation was a subject that virtual strangers often discussed. "I hope you don't mind... What I was doing, I mean?" His brown eyes regarded her steadily, without a trace of self-consciousness or shame.

"No—not at all," she stammered, feeling a hot blush rise in her cheeks and her nipples stiffen involuntarily in her thin black bodice. "It's natural. Everyone does it."

"Do you, Lady Hettie?" he asked softly.

"Please... It's just plain 'Hettie'," she whispered, evading him.

"Hettie." The word was like an intimate caress itself, the way her inquisitor said it. "Hettie, do you touch yourself? Do you give yourself pleasure?"

"I-I—" The answer was locked in her throat. She wanted to tell him but her vocal chords felt as if they were paralyzed.

"I'm sorry, Hettie, I didn't mean to embarrass you," he said quietly. "It's just that I know so little. Or at least I do now... Sex seems to be one of the areas that was blanked by my head injury. It's very frustrating." He bit his full lower lip and something melted inside her. "I'm a man, Hettie, but I can't remember what it's like to be one."

He spoke haltingly, but the expression on his pure, serious face told a clearer story. And for a moment, Hettie felt the maddest urge to try and fill in the gaps for him. He could be hers now if she simply flipped down the straps of her dress, drew him to her naked bosom then lay back and let him take her. She imagined his stiff eager cock rising again, nudging against her, then sliding in. It was only a short while since Starr had pleasured her completely and thoroughly, but astonishingly she already felt like making love again.

Her fingers twitched as if she were really about to loosen her clothing, but then a bell tinkled high and sharply in the corridor outside the library.

"It's the dinner bell," said Hettie as Darryl quirked his

sleek black eyebrows. She felt confused and disorientated. How could she feel attracted to Darryl when Starr's cool, intense presence was becoming more and more imprinted on her consciousness? She glanced at her companion and felt the sharpest pang. He was astonishingly desirable, but acknowledging that desire felt painfully like a betrayal.

And not of her dead husband. Of someone all too living.

Frowning slightly, she watched as Darryl rose smoothly to his feet and held out his arm to her. "Lady Henrietta," he said, his voice formal yet velvety, "may I escort you to dinner?"

Hettie had to smile back at him. He was such a gem. "Of course, *Signor* di Angeli, I'd be honored."

And with that she stood up, took his arm, and let herself be escorted to the dining room.

Starr fell back against the mat, his breathing heavy and his near-naked body streaming with sweat. How many sit-ups had he done? He couldn't remember. He only knew that no amount of hard physical exercise could purge his mind this time.

He lay there for a moment, centering himself, then rose quickly and reached for the bottle of mineral water on the tallboy. Drinking deep, he attempted to focus on his body and gauge his levels of energy and fitness, but all he could really think about was Hettie and what she might be doing with—and saying to—the Italian.

"You're jealous, man," he whispered to himself, then smiled grimly at the enormity of the understatement. He'd seen the way his adored Hettie had looked at di Angeli. And while he'd told himself ferociously that it was not his place to even have an opinion on the matter, he couldn't suppress the gouging surge of sexual envy he experienced each time he'd seen Hettie cast an interested glance at her new houseguest.

Don't be a bloody fool! He took another long drag at the water bottle, then put it aside and peeled off the thin, perspiration-soaked jersey trunks he'd been working out in.

In his tiny bathroom, he spun the showerhead and bared his teeth as he stepped beneath the punishing, brutally ice-cold flow. The water should have dowsed his turbulent emotions and calmed his wayward body, as it so often had before when his longing for Hettie had become unmanageable. But this time the regime was ineffective. His mind and his heart whirled, and despite the confusion of his thoughts and the freezing shower, his cock grew rigid.

"Fuck!" he growled, then spun the dial to a more comfortable temperature. Why suffer when the prescription wasn't working? Why suffer any more than he already was? Than he *always* did.

In his fantasy, the woman he loved, the woman he would do anything for, endure anything for, give anything for, stepped into the cubicle and drew close to him. The now-warm water streamed over her lush but slender body and plastered her lovely mane of golden hair against her skull. Starr groaned like a martyr in torment as a hand closed around his penis. In his dream it was her hand but in reality it was his own.

He had loved Henrietta Miller from the instant he'd first set eyes on her, but if he were to remain an honorable man and worthy of the trust that Piers Miller had placed in him, he could never claim her. He was sworn to protect Hettie and to take care of her—even service her libido when it was required of him—but no more than that. He was her servant and she was his mistress. He knew that his rigid adherence to his role might seem archaic in the twenty-first century, but he'd made a pledge to himself. A pledge in honor of the man who had raised him from the gutter—and from the easy slide into petty, then more serious crime—which he could not break.

The vow was that he would never take advantage of what he and Hettie shared. Never pressure her for more. He wanted and needed her love. It was a glittering prize that shimmered constantly in his imagination. But to pursue it so soon after the death of Piers Miller was to insult his mentor's memory and exploit Hettie's confused emotions and her grief at the loss of her husband. She'd loved Piers deeply, and still loved him. She'd been faithful to him emotionally, even while she'd shared her body with Starr. And that was why he could not claim her.

And yet there was a primitive, territorial part of him that raged to make her his in every way. Heart and soul as well as body. His ancient brain, where instinct held sway, told him that she was his woman and he must imprint himself on every part of her.

I am not a fucking caveman!

He still felt guilt at giving in to his needs the other night. But the urge to show her some physical tenderness after the long months of their mutual celibacy had become too great. And it had finally driven him back to her bed.

His fingers stilled for a moment on his cock at the recollection. He'd barely been able to contain the bittersweet joy he'd experienced when she'd welcomed him. He'd hidden it scrupulously, but as he'd entered her exquisite body, his heart had been singing.

Yes, he was proud of his iron self-discipline, and it never failed him. He couldn't allow it to. Except at private moments like these, when there was nobody but himself and his aching cock to witness his internal agony.

"Oh Hettie, I love you!"

His voice was a ragged, falling cry of longing as her phantom hand rode smoothly back and forth along his engorged rod. His heart twisted as he imagined—remembered—her delicate yet intoxicating touch on his flesh and the way she always and unerringly found the sweetest and most responsive spots. Time after time he'd had to pry her warm fingers off him for fear that he might come in selfishness and not pleasure her at the same time. He'd made yet another oath to himself that his agenda in bed would always be to focus solely on her experience, her satisfaction and her orgasms, even at the expense of his own. If he came in the process, it was a treasured by-product, not the object of the exercise.

But here in this secret zone where wishes could be real, he allowed himself what he denied elsewhere. Here in his imagination, his naked, adorable mistress sank to her knees beneath the cascading water and took his heavy flesh between her moist, caressing lips. Here, it was all right to give in to his every desire and urge and grasp her head, fingers digging into her sensuously coiling hair as he thrust unrestrainedly into the welcoming heat and wetness of her mouth. Here, it was all right to fuck that beautiful mouth, possess that loving, accommodating cavern and then empty his silky load of semen right down her throat.

"Oh Hettie," he cried again, the words a sound of worship, of desperation and of resignation as his creamy tribute hit the shower wall and mingled with the water trickling down it.

"Doesn't *Signor* Starr dine with you?" Darryl asked suddenly over coffee. He'd asked questions. Lots of questions. But Hettie had been both charmed and amused by the subtle way he'd brought her out of herself and finessed information from her. She'd ended up telling him about most of her life, up to and including her marriage to Piers, and was touched by his gentle condolences.

And she didn't mind telling him things. After all, his well of experience had been cruelly emptied. The only way he could find out about life and the world was to hear what'd happened to others.

But this latest question troubled her. As a lot of things about her relationship with Starr did. More and more. Since Piers' death, the dining arrangements had become an issue. She wanted the handsome blond to eat with her. He had insisted—with immaculate but unshakeable politeness—that it was inappropriate and he'd continue to eat alone in his room or in the kitchen.

"He's just 'Starr', and no, he doesn't." She shrugged, wondering for perhaps the hundredth time since they'd sat down just what exactly her cool-eyed protector was doing all this time. "But it's not for want of me asking him." She took a sip of her Amaretto, and savored its fiery almond bite, trying not to dwell on Starr's impenetrable foibles and idiosyncratic standards of what was correct and proper.

"He's a very private man, Darryl, and he likes to observe certain protocols," she continued, swirling her finger around the base of her glass, "Although God knows why he thinks dining with me is improper when he's perfectly happy to—"

Good God, what am I saying?

She hesitated, but Darryl's eyes were wide and bright and his silence tacitly urged her to continue.

"Well, he's a bit more than just a servant, Darryl," she murmured, blushing again.

"I know. I can tell."

"It's... It's difficult to explain. I—" She studied the fine crystal pattern of the glass, unable to face him.

"There's nothing to explain, Hettie," Darryl replied softly, his strange composure throbbing in every syllable. "You need him and you're fond of him, and it's obvious he worships the ground you walk on. And neither of you owe *me* any explanations." His long brown hand slid over her paler, more slender one. "I'm the one who's in debt here. You've let me come into your house when a guest is the last thing you need."

"But, Darryl—"

"It's okay, Hettie," he whispered, stunning her all over again by lifting her hand to his lips.

His mouth barely brushed her skin but it had all the impact of a real kiss.

Hettie bit back a gasp of confusion—as much from the import of Darryl's words as from the contact between his mouth and the back of her hand.

Does Starr worship me?

She knew he felt something for her, but the wall he built between them was so hard to breach. It was so impossible to tell precisely what was going on with him, even in the throes of sexual passion. He almost always cried out her name as he climaxed, but it was never long before he reverted back to his usual respectful yet iron-clad emotional distance. He was like a perfect male robot, programmed to serve her. A beautiful, intuitive, thoughtful and sexually inventive robot certainly, but still one following a very stringent code of conduct.

"Goodnight, Hettie. Please don't think I'm rude, but I feel very tired again."

Hettie snapped back to full consciousness, realizing that Darryl was already taking his leave of her. She'd been so busy wool-gathering about Starr again that she hadn't noticed that Darryl had relinquished her hand and was already on his feet.

"Goodnight, Hettie. And thanks for everything." His gaze flicked down his own body and he grinned impishly, then with a spin like a dancer's he turned and was through the door and gone before she'd even framed her answer.

"What's the matter with me?"

Alone and frustrated, Hettie prowled her room.

What's happening to me?

One day she was a grieving widow, mourning the loss of a husband she'd loved deeply. The next she was some kind of insatiable sexual glutton, experiencing random pangs of lust and totally unable to organize her feelings or formulate any kind of plan that would help her resolve them.

I'll have to say something soon…or I'll go mad!

And yet she hardly dare think about her tall blond servant. Her relationship with him was already mutating faster than she could cope with. Nursing Piers, then mourning him, had allowed her to compartmentalize her peculiar interactions with Starr. But now that the keenest pain of loss was ebbing things weren't so clear-cut.

For her, and maybe for Starr too. She thought about the massage. He'd come to her during the daytime—and taken her so hungrily she could still feel the effects of it.

What was all that about, Mr. Iceman? You broke a rule, Starr. Not mine…one of your own.

The resumption of sex between them had been a huge catalyst. It was no use fooling herself. It wasn't as if she'd stopped missing Piers all of a sudden. She *did* miss him, but she'd been brought back to full sexual life again. She was a mass of surging hunger, and wild to fuck. It was as if she was trying to unconsciously make up for months of celibacy in the space of a few short hours.

And where was Starr tonight when she needed him? He was the one who'd started all this. She'd been assuming he'd visit her room again but as yet there was no sign of him.

Serves me right, Piers, doesn't it? She glanced at her dead husband's photograph as she slipped into a sheer black nightgown, then covered it with a matching floor-length robe. "Two lusty men in the house and neither of them here to service me!" she muttered, half amused, half irritated as she smoothed her fingers over the luxurious silk of her "mourning". Even if the rest of her widowhood was becoming increasingly unconventional, at least she could observe the formality of wearing black.

But Starr might not even be in the house. She'd told Darryl that her servant was a private person and it was nothing but the truth. Starr was also a free agent, and when his duties were done there was nothing to prevent him from going out and leading his own life. His working hours had always been flexible, and neither Piers nor herself had ever expected him to be at their beck and call 24/7. Starr himself was the one who chose to be constantly at her disposal, but theoretically he was free to do what he wanted. He might be visiting friends. He might even have another woman.

No! Please, no!

Hettie sank down onto the bed, winded as if she'd been

rabbit-punched. The thought of Starr with someone else induced a horrid, wrenching twist of jealousy and try as she might to control them, images assailed her. Starr in bed with a woman who wasn't her. A laughing and relaxed Starr, fucking for himself and not because he felt duty-bound to service his employer.

Hettie had no way of knowing whether Starr maintained other relationships because he'd never once told her anything of his life beyond his employment in the Miller household.

Dare she go to him? That was another thing she'd never done. Only once during Piers' illness had she suggested that she might visit Starr in his rooms. But that suggestion had been quashed with infinite tact and politeness. Starr was at her command and he would come to her.

"Well, bullshit to that! This is my house and I do what I want!" muttered Hettie, cinching the sash of her robe more tightly and leaping to her feet again. She slipped out of her bedroom and made her way silently towards the staircase leading to the upper floors, mentally psyching herself up as she went.

What if he wasn't there? What if he didn't want her in his room? Invading his only private, personal space in the home that belonged to her. On the landing, a few yards from his door, she hesitated, gnawing her lower lip. Oh, Starr would be polite to her, as calm and cool and amenable as always. He would probably even willingly accompany her back to her room and make love to her. But she would always suspect he was only doing it because she'd forced the issue.

Her body shaking, and feeling a horrid sensation of cowardice, she backed away from Starr's door and turned to go back the way she'd come. But as she did so, she noticed another door slightly ajar.

It was hot and stuffy in the old set of "nanny's rooms"

that hadn't been used since Piers had bought the house a few years ago. Nobody had opened the windows in ages and there was dust on the furniture and fittings, but the closed circuit TV system that'd once been used to monitor the nursery was still in full working order.

When Hettie switched it on, the image was surprisingly sharp for a not so young piece of equipment—and it was of the room that had once been a nursery but was now one of the guestrooms. Wearing an unbelted robe and toweling his jet-black hair, Darryl walked slowly into the camera's all-seeing range and paused as if he knew she was watching him.

After a few moments, he tossed aside his towel, shucked off his robe and turned fully towards the camera, his hands rising elegantly to sweep back his tousled hair. Then he spread out his arms, stretched hugely, and as his naked body arched towards her, Hettie swallowed, her own body instantly stirring.

It was as if he were displaying himself to her. She gasped, feeling sweat trickle between her breasts and her pussy fluttering in the age-old female response to masculine beauty.

Darryl was skinny and sleek, just as she'd imagined him. An exquisite Adonis, smooth of chest and lightly muscled but with a cock between his shining thighs that was sturdy and impressive.

Goddammit, he's nearly as big as Starr! Her hand flew unconsciously to her crotch.

He wasn't fully erect yet, but Hettie could see that was about to change. She dropped into a chair beside the console, still watching, then reached for the contrast control. As the image sharpened, she saw Darryl lie down, stretch out his long brown limbs on the bed, then slowly and languidly reach down and take hold of his cock.

She watched entranced as he first pumped himself to

a complete imposing hardness, then let his fingers stray luxuriously over the rest of his body. Slowly and at leisure, he touched his belly, his chest and his thighs—and then when he pinched his nipples, his hips bucked upward and his penis swayed spectacularly.

Hettie felt her own sex boil. Fulminating, it called on a primal, purely physical level to his penis, wanting it inside her. How would it be to climb onto that bed, kneel over Darryl's slim silky body, and lower herself onto him?

She imagined him filling her and stretching her, pushing up into her, thrusting hard and fast and battering the mouth of her womb. His long drives would pull on her clitoris and in seconds she'd be spasming and moaning and clasping his cock with the wet, yielding walls of her channel.

And as—on the monitor—his fingers returned to his genitals, so—in the darkness of the old nanny's bedroom—did Hettie's fly urgently to hers.

Lifting the shimmering fall of her skirt, she arranged the delicate cloth in folds at her waist and eased her legs apart. As Darryl stroked the tip of his cock, stimulating the most sensitive part of his body, Hettie mirrored him by touching her fingertip to the most delicate and responsive area of hers. There was moisture in abundance in her sex and she smoothed it copiously over her clitoris, imagining it was the hand of her gorgeous houseguest that was anointing her.

"Oh God… Oh yes…please…" She moaned, then froze as the monitor showed her that he too was muttering. With her free hand she reached out to turn up the volume switch while the other resumed its delicate manipulation of her clitoris.

Husky groans filled the room, the raw sound of a horny man uninhibitedly enjoying his own body.

His noises were indecipherable at first, indistinct sighs

and grunts and fragments of both English and Italian. But as he cradled his balls in one hand and stroked his streaming red shaft with the other, one clear unmistakable utterance seemed to fly out of the speaker and caress Hettie's sex like a living, tangible entity.

"Hettie! Oh Hettie!" he cried, his voice musical yet strangled as his hips lurched up from the bed beneath him and milk-white semen jetted out from between his working fingers and flew in an arc through the air.

"Oh you sweet thing!" she gasped fondly as her own body gave itself up to pleasure and her clitoris danced beneath her touch. With her eyes locked on the jerking figure on the screen, she felt her pussy flex and pulse as if it were trying to grab the stiff dark thing that he held so tightly in his fist.

"Oh God, yes! Yes!" she whimpered, coming superbly, but also painfully aware that she was empty and she needed to be filled. That it wasn't her new visitor that she wanted to share these moments with, but someone else. Someone who was close by, but as distant in some ways as the stars he was named for...

Darryl's orgasm seemed to go on and on, his semen flying out into the empty air. Hettie panted, pulsing with him, her pussy a mass of quivering fire yet desperate for full penetration.

With a long moan, she detached her consciousness from his, closing her eyes tightly and slumping back into her chair, her bottom still wriggling convulsively against the plush upholstery beneath her. She was still coming slightly, her own body amazing her with both its power and its insatiable need and hunger.

But suddenly and incredibly, a facet of that hunger was satisfied. Two fingers slid into her empty channel. Two solid male fingers that filled her aching void and made a firm, sure foundation for the strong flat thumb that nudged her hovering fingers aside and settled fairly and squarely on her clitoris.

Hettie howled like an animal as her orgasm flared anew, then soared to an almost unbearable peak of sensation. Rapture consumed her, ecstasy drained her and there was no strength left to either lift her heavy eyelids or frame her brain around the words of a question.

As her belly beat and fluttered she felt a warm mouth settle there and kiss her, the touch of it so tender that her heart almost broke in gratitude. Then the fingers were plunging deeper into her, matching the rhythm of her flesh, their motion smooth in her wet silkiness as the thumb remained steady on her clitoris. Hettie's legs flailed helplessly, her bare feet striking her caresser's body again and again as she jerked and cried out in her climax.

It seemed a long, long time before her pussy stilled and her limbs lay loose and at rest. Splayed and bared, with her sex still glowing, she felt the one who'd pleasured her rise from between her legs, then heard a tiny click as the monitor was turned off and the post orgasmic Darryl was consigned to privacy and presumably his sleep.

Hettie's own limbs felt like lead and her body devoid of all energy. All she could manage was a sigh of contentment when she was picked up in a pair of powerful arms and carried from the room like a feather-light doll.

It was only when she was laid gently on her own bed and the strong hands that had held and caressed her started exploring her body again, that she finally came back to her senses. Thrills shot along her nerves as her robe and nightgown were quickly and efficiently stripped off and her thighs were taken hold of and eased apart.

And as she felt the hard, warm head of a penis against

her wetness, and the beginnings of a slow, determined push, Hettie finally managed to open her eyes. Open them and look straight up into Starr's calm, blue and unswerving gaze.

"My lady," he whispered, but before she could form an answer, his mouth plunged down on hers and his cock slid home.

Whatever she might have said to him was forgotten.

Chapter Four

"Why not ask Doctor Madrigan?"

Like everything Starr suggested, it was sensible, rational and probably the right thing to do. But sitting here in a chic Harley Street waiting room, Hettie wasn't even sure quite what she wanted to ask. Precise questions hadn't been an issue in the still, sweaty hours of the previous night.

After they'd made love—or she'd been "made love to"—she'd felt relaxed enough to air some of her general concerns over Darryl to Starr. In the cold light of day, she probably wouldn't have voiced them but at night, feeling warm and loose in Starr's arms, it had seemed as natural as breathing to seek his opinion on what to do to help her amnesiac guest.

The fact that he'd discovered her watching Darryl masturbate was not mentioned. Just like the fact that she and Starr had begun having sex again, it was clearly a nonissue and not to be discussed. At least not if Starr had his way.

But she was going to have to discuss it with Stevie. Which was why she'd come to Harley Street.

Stephanie Madrigan was a medical doctor turned counselor who Hettie had consulted in the confused days of Piers' illness when she'd been torn between her own irrepressible libido and her devotion to her increasingly impotent husband.

It was surely no coincidence that the answer to that dilemma—Starr—was the solution that Stevie had so delicately and sensitively hinted at even before Piers had proposed it himself. And if she'd been right last time, there was no reason to believe that she wouldn't have a sound suggestion this time.

So yes, an appointment with Doctor Stevie was the most logical course of action. Sort of…

"The doctor will see you now, Lady Henrietta."

The receptionist's pleasant voice broke into Hettie's inner debate and set up a little flutter in her heart.

Stevie's therapy methods sometimes led to soul-searching and unearthed difficult facts that had to be faced.

Hettie smoothed down her skirt as she rose to her feet and followed the girl into the consulting room. And as a slender and rather dapper figure rose from behind the desk and came forward to meet her, she experienced a glow of pleasure coupled with a strange forbidden thrill.

Doctor Stephanie Madrigan was handsome woman of medium height whose sleekly gelled auburn hair and elegant clothing were as severe and masculine as her perfectly appointed consulting room. She'd been a friend of Piers and had become Hettie's friend too.

"How are you, Hettie?" the doctor inquired, her soft voice seeming to flow across Hettie like honey as she led the way to a leather-covered sofa. "I've been wanting to come and visit you, but I thought I'd better wait until you were ready. Please, won't you sit down?" Her firm hand guided Hettie down onto the deeply upholstered couch. "Let's have a glass of sherry, shall we? I'm sure it's not too early, and it's not as if this is a formal consultation, is it?"

Hettie watched her pour two glasses of fine old sherry from a cut glass decanter on the sideboard, then place them on a small occasional table before them. She suddenly realized that she hadn't yet spoken a word.

That was the effect Stevie Madrigan had on her, born of the realization that the doctor's kindly and professional persona held in check some openly bisexual sentiments. Sentiments that always piqued Hettie's sensual curiosity.

"Now then, how can I help?"

A dozen answers hovered on Hettie's lips but none of them quite made sense. Now that she was in the consulting room she didn't really know why she was here. Ostensibly, it was Darryl, but in her heart it was Starr she was consulting Stevie's wisdom about.

"Well, it's like this," she began haltingly, "I got a phone call from a friend the other night. Renata di Angeli, I think you know her... She asked me if her cousin could come and stay with me."

Quickly and with more ease than Hettie had expected, the whole story came pouring out. Darryl. His beauty. The pangs of attraction she'd felt. All the while Hettie spoke, she was aware of Stevie's piercing eyes upon her, occasionally narrowing as if the doctor was hearing far more than the words that Hettie occasionally faltered over. When the newly resumed nocturnal visits from Starr were finally revealed, Stevie tapped her forefinger sagely against the side of her elegant nose. She'd listened in silence until that moment, but now she gave a soft and kindly laugh.

"So at last we reach the *real* reason you're here." Stevie's eyes glittered as she poured more sherry.

"What do you mean?" demanded Hettie, gulping her sherry and only just managing not to splutter. "I came here to ask you about Darryl, not Starr. Starr and I have an arrangement. It's perfectly civilized. It doesn't need discussing. It just works."

"Rubbish!" announced the doctor crisply. "The sex part works okay, naturally. How could it not work with a hunk like him? No, it's more than that. The man adores you. Haven't you realized that by now? And he always has done. And that, my dear, beautiful, sexy Hettie, is why Piers threw the two of you together in the first place. He was looking ahead, bless him—" Stevie's face contorted a moment, in obvious sorrow. Piers had been her lover too, some years before Hettie and he had met. "He was grooming Starr as his full-time replacement, after his death."

Hettie did splutter then, and she was pink in the face by the time Stevie had brought her a drink of water from the cooler in the corner of the room.

"But how can Starr love me?" protested Hettie when she was able to speak clearly again. "I mean... He's passionate enough in bed, but he never actually says very much. And out of bed, well, he's...he's...so correct. So distant. So goddamned bloody *polite*! It's like having a ten-foot brick wall between us all the time!"

For a moment an intense and almost painful longing gripped her heart. She imagined low, fevered endearments murmured in that deep, yet melodic voice of his. Protestations of affection, and—even more exquisite—avowals of devotion and love.

Oh, Starr! A sheen of tears suddenly clouded her eyes.

"Of course he hasn't said anything," said Stevie, sounding exasperated. "He's bound himself into some ridiculous and archaic code of honor and chivalry where you're concerned, Hettie. It's some sort of demented, half-assed reverse version of 'courtly adoration' where he'll fuck your brains out but he'll never reveal that he loves you!"

"But why?"

Hettie abandoned her water and reached for her sherry again. She felt more confused than ever by this confirmation of something she had sort of suspected. And hoped for.

Does Starr love me?

Was he hiding profound emotions beneath that faultless façade of courtesy and service? What she'd told Stevie had been true. Although he expressed his pleasure at the peak of their couplings, sometimes in low heartfelt groans, sometimes in hoarse shouts, sometimes in colorful profanities—he never ever spoke actual words of love.

Which made him seem even more superhuman than ever. How could a man love a woman and share the most intense physical intimacies with her yet not disclose his feelings?

It didn't seem possible, even for an exceptional personality like Starr.

"I think you're wrong, Stevie," Hettie said, frowning. "Surely he would have told me if he felt like that? How could he not?"

Suddenly, Hettie experienced a great swirl of emotion. What kind of a mess was she in? What did *she* feel? She cared for Starr, she knew that, and knew it was *more* than that. He was beginning to dominate her thoughts for virtually all her waking hours. And even her dreams sometimes.

Was that love? Or just a deep bond of reliance and sexual tenderness because of the situation they'd found themselves in?

"Because he's Starr," said Stevie, "And he's a stubborn so-and-so, and he won't break a rule. Even if he's the one who's made it."

Hettie felt like hugging her arms around herself and

rocking with distress. *What am I going to do? What am I going to do?*

"Hey, relax, don't get upset." Stevie's voice was soft, and soothing, and it was only then that Hettie realized that she actually *was* rocking and was hunched forward, clutching her sherry glass as if her life depended on it.

The doctor pried Hettie's fingers from around the glass and put it aside. A moment later, her slender arm slid around Hettie's shoulders, instantly imparting a welcome sensation of comfort and reassurance. "What am I going to do?" whispered Hettie, unable to prevent herself from leaning into Stevie's warm, calming hold.

Stevie let out a sigh. "Maybe you just need to stop worrying and trying to analyze what might happen," she said softly, "and just relax and *let* things happen." Stevie shook her head and tut-tutted. "Men, eh? They're splendid creatures…but they're trouble too. What you need right now is a complete change of scene. A chance to kick back and relax away from the city."

"But I can't relax!" Hettie cried, more confused than ever, "How can I? I've suddenly turned into a sex maniac!" Shaking, she huddled close and hid her face against Stevie's shoulder, "I'm a widow, for God's sake! It seems obscene to be so horny at a time like this! And yet when Starr turned up the other night, it was suddenly *exactly* what I wanted!" She bit her lip, wondering again how the cool, unfathomable blond had known to come to her room anyway.

"Actually," said Stevie, her other arm circling around Hettie too, making an embrace that was both comforting and vaguely sensual at the same time. "Your increased sex drive is quite natural at a time like this."

Unable to stop herself, Hettie looked into Stevie's eyes again and found them steady and intent. The other woman's gaze made her feel settled again.

"You've suffered a great loss, Hettie," Stevie went on. "Had a close brush with death. And now your mind and your body are reaching out to life again. In the simplest and most straightforward way." Her long fingers moved gently and soothingly over Hettie's back. "Sex is life, Hettie. What's happening is your soul's own way of healing itself. You mustn't try to fight it."

"But I don't fight it!" Hettie gave a rueful grin as relaxation flooded through her. "I'm ready the moment Starr steps through the bedroom door. Before even. Sometimes I only have to look at the back of his head when he's driving me somewhere and I want him!"

Stevie answered the grin, her hand stilling on Hettie's back. "And there's nothing wrong with that. But are you sure it's just desire you feel for him?"

Of course it isn't. It's much more. I love him.

The words sprang into her mind, unbidden, but somehow they stalled behind her lips. She dragged in a deep, deep breath as if the wind had been knocked out of her. And as she stared at Stevie in confusion, the image of the doctor was blurred by sudden tears. A moment ago she'd felt calm, but now she was all over the place again, thrown into chaos by thoughts of a pair of cool, unreadable blue eyes and the irrational effect they had on her heart and her body.

Great sobs made her shake and gasp for air again, but Stevie's arms closed even tighter, kept her still. "There, there," the doctor murmured, whispering gentle soothing nonsense in Hettie's ear as she shuddered and wept.

It took a while, but eventually the storm inside Hettie blew itself out. She unwound herself from Stevie's hold and heaved a sigh, still perplexed but calmer now.

"But I loved Piers. I still love him. How can I already be

having feelings for someone else?"

Stevie shrugged her elegant shoulders, and patted Hettie's hand. With a wry little smile, she reached for a box of tissues from the coffee table and handed them to her. "There isn't a straightforward answer to that one, love. But I do know that what you're feeling isn't wrong. And you know that Piers wouldn't think it was wrong, don't you?"

Hettie nodded, thinking of her kindly husband, whose love had been more generous and more selfless than any woman deserved. She dabbed her eyes, feeling drained. Wishing that there were a way to take time out, and just think about everything.

"It's all too much. I can't take it in." The tissue was turning to shreds in her hands now, and without speaking, Stevie reached for a wastepaper basket beside the chair and held it out.

"Piers. Starr. Now Darryl too. I don't know what to do. I feel completely muddled." Hettie tossed the tissue in the bin. "What would you do, oh wise one?" She found herself smiling, suddenly seeing absurdity in her situation.

"Okay, here's the thing," the doctor said at last. "Like I said, you need to get away from the city and take a holiday down at Dragonwood. You. Starr. Darryl. A nice, relaxing break in the country air... Just what the doctor ordered!"

Stevie grinned, looking mightily pleased with her prescription. Reaching for the sherry, she topped off both their glasses a little. "And if I can fix it, I'll come down there too, and I'll take care of your horny Italian for you. How does that sound? If I assume the responsibility for 'educating' Darryl, that'll leave you free to sort out exactly where you stand with Starr. And get things out in the open at last." She took a sip of sherry and regarded Hettie sharply over the rim of her glass. "You know it needs to be done."

"Do you really think so?" Hettie asked, feeling a surge of confidence.

"I know so!" said Stevie decisively. "And I think the best way to do it is to give all the staff down there some paid leave, so we can all just fend for ourselves. And keep things intimate."

"Yes, you're right!"

A great excitement welled up inside Hettie, a fluttering in her heart not unlike the sensation long ago when she'd been planning her honeymoon with Piers. They'd stayed at Dragonwood then, in love with the beauty and atmosphere of the exquisite Queen Anne pocket mansion as much as they were with each other. Not that they'd seen much of the house. The room they'd become most thoroughly acquainted with had been the bedroom.

But this time, it would be Starr sharing that bedroom. And this time it was *his* heart she'd delve in to and decipher. Even if she didn't like what she found there, she had to know. Or go crazy.

"It's perfect!" cried Stevie, clearly warming to her theme now and gesturing gaily to the sunshine that was streaming in through the window. "In this weather you can go native too. Swim and sunbathe naked. If that doesn't start things happening I don't know what will!"

It was a wonderful idea, although Hettie decided not to point out that she always preferred not to get *too* much sun. But it didn't matter. There was a lovely trellis-shaded terrace at the side of the house, close to the outdoor pool, where she could bask on a lounge chair and enjoy the fresh air without getting baked. Starr, of course, was magnificently tanned, his muscular body like beaten gold all over, and she didn't imagine the heat would bother Darryl too much either. He was already sun-kissed and his skin the color of honeyed caramel.

"Mmm…" Hettie looked closely at Stevie and saw her eyes were glittering brilliantly as if pure devilish glee had been shot through an emerald prism.

"You know you might try flirting with Darryl. It might take something drastic like a bit of old-fashioned macho jealousy to melt Starr's ice and force him into telling you exactly how he feels."

"Stevie! You are outrageous! You can't seriously be suggesting that!"

"Why not! It's worth a shot. And don't try and tell me it hasn't already crossed your mind."

Hettie blushed. As ever, Stevie was bang on target.

"Or you could always flirt with me?" the doctor suggested.

"Stevie!" Hettie protested again, but less vehemently. Stevie had a knack of employing this kind of harmless sexual teasing between them to lift the mood. But for a second, Hettie did wonder. Wonder what might have happened in a world where Starr didn't exist…

"I'm only fooling with you," said Stevie gently. "You've got to lighten up a bit and not be so hard on yourself all the time." Her beautiful face grew suddenly solemn. "But seriously, as for Starr, you know he'd do anything in the world that you asked of him, don't you? Including laying down his life if it came to it."

She'd never actually thought about it, but as Stevie said it Hettie knew it was true. "Yes, I know he would. But I don't think he'd admit to jealousy even if he *felt* it. He's the most private man I've ever met. Which is exactly the problem."

"That's as may be. But let's get back to the matter in hand. Where exactly are the men in your life today, by the way?"

"Well, Darryl was still fast asleep when I left, so I just left him to have a lie-in. I feel a bit of a selfish bitch though.

I should have been showing him the sights of London or something. Being a good hostess. Taking proper care of him." Hettie gnawed her lip, feeling guilty that her obsession with her own emotional problems seemed to have eclipsed those of her Italian visitor.

"Don't panic, love," Stevie said gently. "He's probably better off taking it easy just now. He's had a trauma and some big changes in his life, and it'll take some getting used to."

Hettie described Darryl's persistent tiredness, then suddenly found herself telling Stevie what she'd seen last night, just before Starr had come and whisked her out of the nanny's room. The image of Darryl collapsing back onto the bed, his body loose, boneless and sated. His orgasm preparing him for rest.

"That's good," Stevie said, apparently completely unfazed by the idea of Hettie's voyeurism. "It means his constitution his trying to heal itself naturally. The more rest he gets the better, and we all know what activity promotes the deepest relaxation and the most beneficial sleep, don't we?"

"Yes," said Hettie, thinking of long warm days at Dragonwood, of curtains fluttering in a bedroom, and after-sex drowsiness and sweaty bodies still entwined. But the male form was a familiar one not her new houseguest. "And I'll do what you say. Take him to the country where he can get it. Rest, I mean! Fresh air and sleep... Whatever!" she retorted in answer to Stevie's mischievous look.

She smiled though, as she looked at her friend, and wondered what lay ahead of them.

She was going away for a country house party... With Starr, Darryl *and* Stevie.

She didn't dare begin to predict the outcome.

Chapter Five

Hettie's sense of fatalistic anticipation lasted all the rest of that day and into the next one.

Traveling home from Stevie's consulting rooms, she tried to focus on the practicalities of the coming trip to Dragonwood rather than the welter of confused emotions that that tumbled in her mind. But it was difficult.

What do I feel for Starr? How can I love a man so remote and so emotionally buttoned-up?

And if she *did* love him, how was it she could also find Darryl such a turn-on too?

Putting aside her questions for a moment, she reviewed the plans for their trip. They could drive down in the big car tomorrow morning. Herself, Darryl and Starr at the wheel of course. Stevie, after clearing her appointment schedule, would follow around lunchtime.

Starr would make any necessary staffing arrangements and Hettie knew better than to interfere in that area. He was managing her household perfectly well without any assistance from her whatsoever, and she suspected he'd be mortally offended if she started trying to stick her nose in and make changes. She knew that eventually she'd take hold of the reins of her life again, and think about a productive future and perhaps returning to gallery work, but now was not the time.

When she arrived at Pengilley Gardens, she was relieved to find she needn't have worried about Darryl being left alone.

"Oh, he's gone off with Mister Starr, milady," Mrs. Phillips informed her cheerfully. "Gone to the British Museum, I believe."

I wonder if they talked about me.

Hettie sorted through the clothes she would take to Dragonwood, feeling relieved that the two men were getting on together, even while natural curiosity drove her crazy. They'd probably just discuss the exhibits, she decided, tossing a pile of delicate underwear into her suitcase. Starr would rather have his tongue cut out and be tortured on the rack rather than reveal any of their personal business to a relative stranger. No, *she* was always the one who'd always told tales out of the bedroom.

Still packing—first putting items in, then taking them out again—she thought of the days of Piers' illness and the times she'd described to him the things that Starr had done to her between the sheets. It was a kind of conveyed voyeurism, wasn't it?

And she knew perfectly well that Starr had been fully aware of her erotic accounts of his performances. She'd often suspected he'd done some slightly more exotic things than were normal just so she'd have something particularly spicy to tell Piers. He was a modest man, solemn and unassuming, but there was a certain quiet grandeur to him and Hettie rather suspected that he was proud of his supreme performances in bed.

And well you might be!

When Darryl returned he was full of praise for the British Museum. Hettie wondered as he spoke enthusiastically and knowledgeably of the various exhibits whether the antiquarian atmosphere had triggered any memories for him. Yet she saw no signs of distress or pondering. No sign that he was racking his brain. If he was beginning to recall his former life with his archaeologist uncle the memories were obviously easier now.

Over a quiet dinner she told him about the trip to Dragonwood and its informal nature.

"I'd like that very much, Hettie," he said quietly, his expression suddenly very straight and incisive.

"Yes, it'll be fun, won't it?"

Hettie took a sip of her fizzy water to cover her confusion. *He's got that expression again.* She placed the glass down again very carefully. *It's as if he's reading my mind. As if he knows exactly why we're going there!*

"It'll just be quiet though. Just you and me and Starr and a friend I was with today. You'll like her. Doctor Madrigan. She's been giving me some bereavement counseling. She's very good."

She was babbling. And telling white lies. It'd never been her widowhood she'd consulted Stevie about, and she had a sudden very vivid impression that Darryl was fully aware of that fact.

"I look forward to meeting her," he said softly, his smile exquisitely intriguing and his brown eyes bright.

I just bet you do! Hettie trembled slightly as she turned her attention to a dinner she was too perplexed to eat.

The evening had ended strangely. A simple throwaway goodnight kiss from Darryl had set Hettie's senses aflame, kindling the sexual heat in her that seemed to be simmering all the time now.

"Goodnight, Hettie," he'd said, walking around to her where she still sat at table. He'd looked a picture, all in dark blue, in a soft silk shirt and Italian-tailored trousers. He was so handsome and so easy to want that under any other circumstances, she might simply have propositioned him. Especially when he leaned forward and pressed his lips against her burning cheek.

Nephews kissed aunts like this, and favorite grandsons put their mouths this lightly and slightly to the cheeks of their grandmas. But to Hettie it was a trigger, launching a wave of sexual energy that swept over her belly, her breasts, and her pussy. It was over in seconds and she was stunned. And afterward she couldn't even remember if she'd actually said goodnight back to him.

Later in the darkness, she couldn't sleep. She lay thinking of her body's extreme reaction to Darryl's innocent kiss and of Stevie's advice and everything they'd discussed. Her senses were primed and she longed for Starr's arrival.

Are you even going to turn up?

A glance at the illuminated clock revealed a late, late hour. Surely he'd have come by now if he were going to. Throwing back the covers, Hettie prepared to do something she'd almost done last night—go to Starr's rooms and seek him out—but at that very moment, the door slid almost soundlessly open and a tall figure appeared in her room.

Greetings and questions clamored in her throat yet faced with him Hettie could not utter a word. She simply watched as he moved forward through the shadows and approached her bed. There was a glimmer of moonlight through the partially closed curtains, and it seemed to paint his long, muscular body with silver as he swiftly shed his robe.

If only I could see your eyes.

The plea remained silent though as he lifted the bedcover and took his place beside her.

If only I could see what's in your heart.

But the moonbeams weren't sufficient to reveal him and his face and his amazing blue eyes remained frustratingly shadowed.

I must ask him! I must know how he feels!

The questions tormented her as he efficiently stripped away her nightgown, then ran a long hand down the full length of her torso, lingering at breast and hip. She opened her mouth, not knowing what she was going to say, but before she could utter a word, he covered it with his hand. The same hand that had shaped her curves settled gently but firmly over her lips, sealing her to silence.

In the darkness, he seemed fierce, almost like angry primal man forbidding his woman to speak. And then a second later the hand was gone. Only to be replaced by Starr's mouth, kissing her with a new and unprecedented savagery as if he wanted to expunge any words that might come between them.

Starr, what is it? Do you love me...or hate me?

Her cries remained unuttered as she thrilled to the animal intensity of the kiss. Her jaw ached. She felt as if he were devouring her as his tongue explored and possessed the delicate interior of her mouth. And as he kissed ferociously, his hand slid between her legs, taking possession there too. He caressed her thrillingly, rubbing quite hard and occasionally edging back and forcing her legs wider so he could gain better access.

As she groaned around his tongue, he pushed first one,

then two, then three fingers inside her, thrusting and rocking them until her besieged flesh yielded its pleasure to him and she climaxed so intensely it was almost painful.

A second later, he was inside her, his cock as insistent and dominating as his fingers had been. He powered into her, the strokes deep and angry. Instinctively, she rose to him, glorying in his loving ruthlessness and orgasming again quickly and violently.

Her mind was a maelstrom of pure feeling, but at the edge of consciousness, she still heard the desperation in Starr's hoarse cry of release.

Was that true emotion he was expressing? Or simply the physical, as ever, overwhelming him? Exhaustion overcame her before she was able to determine…

When Hettie woke up, she still felt troubled and frustrated despite the fact that Starr had made love to her so beautifully in the night.

After his first onslaught, she'd slept. But on waking several times, she'd discovered him still with her and he'd taken her again, each time quashing her attempts at communication with his lips or the power of his body.

And yet still she felt horny. She considered masturbating, but the height of the sun in the sky said she'd slept quite late and the sooner she got up, the sooner they could set off for Dragonwood.

A soft knock at the door heralded Starr with her morning tea.

It always amazed her how he could behave with such detached politeness in the morning, when the night before he'd fucked her into mindlessness.

"I trust you slept well, ma'am," he said quietly, lightening her strong morning brew with just the right amount of milk.

"Yes, thank you, Starr. Is everything ready for the trip?" she answered briskly. In the harsh light of day it seemed impossible to ask him anything at all. Impossible to attempt anything other than the normal, mannered relationship they maintained during daylight hours.

But in her heart, she cried out passionately.

How do you feel, Starr? How do you really feel? What do I mean to you?

But for the moment she felt shackled by their unspoken rule, in which neither of them ever admitted that their relationship was other than mistress and servant. It was impossible to force the words from her lips.

"Yes, ma'am. The cases are loaded and Darryl is having his breakfast now. He seems to be looking forward to the trip."

Hettie looked at him sharply. Had there been just the tiniest hint of an edge in his voice? Was the man carved from granite laughing at her?

Or maybe really *was* he jealous?

Hettie's senses leapt. She swallowed a huge gasp, fighting a wash of panicked emotion. It was too much to hope for. She was probably imagining things.

"So am I," she said as evenly as she could, calling what might be an imagined bluff. "I'm hoping it'll be a very productive stay. Educational even, perhaps?" Perhaps if she challenged him again and again, as much as she could, she could break through that solid marble wall of his?

"Very possibly."

But there was nothing. Not even the merest crimp of his perfectly sculpted lips or the faintest flash of green envy in his crystal blue eyes. "If there's any way I can assist you, milady, please let me know."

Hettie felt her nipples harden and was grateful for the sheet tucked up under her armpits.

"Any way at all?" she inquired, her voice bland but her heart pounding and leaping.

"Anything," he said softly, the lack of an honorific telling her that in a rare daytime moment, he was speaking to the woman and not the employer.

"I may just take you up on that." She smiled as calmly as she could and reached for her tea. "Now I'd better get this drunk and get my act together. Time's passing and we've got a fair journey ahead of us."

"We certainly have, ma'am," murmured Starr as he turned on his heel and left her to her morning routine.

Leaving Hettie wondering just exactly what kind of journey he was referring to.

Hettie dressed very carefully to travel. Two days ago she'd just flung on a shirt and jeans to meet Darryl and ride in a car with him, but now she felt he was at least worthy of her making an effort and she adorned herself appropriately.

She was also aware of another, more compelling agenda. The simple desire to always look beautiful for Starr...

Her two-piece was black figured silk, with a full and swirling skirt and a matching top that flattered her breasts to perfection.

She tried in on first with a bra and then without. It was unsubtle of course, but she felt sensitized and sexual. She wanted to be more aware of her body than she would have been if all neatly trussed up in a bra. She had no doubt that both Darryl and Starr would enjoy the view, and that the tall blond would notice the younger man's looks of admiration.

Stevie had talked about making Starr jealous in an attempt to compel him to reveal his feelings. Hettie wasn't so sure about that tactic, but now that it was floating around somewhere in her subconscious she couldn't ignore it. She had no intention of openly flirting with Darryl, because that would be unkind to both the men. But perhaps if Starr saw her houseguest making eyes at her, it might force him to rethink his own emotional repression, and consider the possibility that if he didn't make a move, one day someone else would.

But then again, you might just suck it up and go on with your Mr. Cool Faultless Perfect Servant act, mightn't you, you stubborn bastard?

Sighing, Hettie returned her attention her appearance.

After fluffing out her glossy hair, she painted her eyelids with a smoky shadow and stained her lips with cranberry pink. In her widow's weeds, she knew she'd never looked better.

The men's reactions were thrilling. Her body stirred with both excitement and a strange fear when Starr's blue laser gaze raked her from head to foot in a way she'd never seen before. His demeanor out of the bedroom had always been the acme of perfect respect and discretion. He'd never once appeared to ogle her, even when she'd been going out with Piers and wearing the most risqué of cocktail dresses. But now his eyes were incendiary and seemed to possess every part of her, rendering the black silk ensemble transparent and revealing every inch of her intimate flesh. Hettie felt that it was the real man responding to her at last, the man *behind* the mask acknowledging her beauty and her desirability, his amazing eyes referring directly to what they shared when they had sex together.

Darryl was simply thunderstruck, his beautiful mouth dropping open in wonder and staying that way for a full ten seconds.

"Wow! You look amazing, Hettie," he said, his voice awed and his eyes like hot coals. His body seemed suddenly tense as if acutely uncomfortable. Hettie could almost taste him wanting her. It was like a vapor in the air, thickening in intensity as they climbed into the back seat of the car together and the door was closed to seal them in a private world.

Hettie smiled, a little nervously, and thanked Darryl for the compliment.

I've made a mistake, haven't I? Her body seemed to tingle under his scrutiny. *I should have worn jeans after all. This is all too much.* She twitched her skirt over her knees and shifted uneasily in her seat.

As if to deliberately make matters worse, Starr pushed a button and the tinted glass barrier rose up between him and his passengers. Hettie felt a pang of loss and then a rush of intense, female anger at him. He'd deliberately detached himself from her all over again.

Sitting in such an enclosed space with Darryl was like being in a pressure cooker. He wasn't Starr, but he was near. *Too* near. And the scent of him, and the sudden tension, made her feel a bit dizzy. It was a familiar cologne—light and spicy—but she couldn't put a name to it. She doubted if she could put a name to anything right now, her mind was in such a jumble.

"How long will it take?" Darryl said suddenly as the car began its glide through the London streets, guided by Starr's experienced hand.

Will what take?

Hettie felt blood warm her face and throat. The question had caught her unaware, but she realized now it was an innocent enquiry. It was only in her mind that it had acquired significant overtones.

"A couple of hours," she said, schooling her voice to casualness, "More if there are roadworks anywhere. Less if Starr's feeling lucky. He likes to make the car earn its keep, so to speak. But don't worry, he's an expert driver. We're quite safe."

Safe on the road, she added silently, knowing that there was a different kind of danger in sitting next to a hot-blooded man in tight jeans and a chest-hugging T-shirt.

Especially when I can't stop thinking about sex!

To distract herself, she launched into a sudden nervous description of the house they were heading for. She knew that she sounded like a robotic stately home tour guide, but the flow of words was a soothing distraction from her turbulent thoughts and feelings.

Whether Darryl understood her tactics or not she had no way of knowing, but he listened attentively nevertheless.

Dragonwood was a modest Queen Anne house, set in its own park and halfway between the South Downs coast and the village of Melton Parva. Talking about it was a therapy to Hettie, and as the car snaked its way steadily out of the metropolis, the images in her mind of the elegant pale-stoned building calmed her. Her pulse steadied as she cataloged its many joys and treasures—the warm-toned wood-paneled rooms, the paintings and furniture, the library full of rare and precious books, the gardens full of flowers and shrubs and trees.

"Can you swim, Darryl?" she asked him presently. "There's a lovely pool."

"I-I think so." He hesitated, frowning, and Hettie realized

he honestly didn't remember. She felt a surge of pity and without thinking, reached out to touch his bare arm. What a nightmare, not to know what you'd done and what you'd learned. Even who you were, really.

Surprisingly her touch didn't seem to startle him. His hand and arm remained still and warm beneath her fingers, but he raised the other and started rubbing at a small area of his forehead. He frowned again, his smooth face crumpling in a way that Hettie found worrying.

"Are you okay?" she asked, her own fingers tightening on his forearm.

"Yes, thanks, I'm fine." He smiled at her, slightly wan beneath his tan. "It's just when I try too hard to remember things, I get a bit of a headache sometimes." His fingers still circled at his forehead. "But I'm almost certain that I *can* swim!" He looked tired but quite pleased with himself, as if remembering a simple, everyday skill was a major achievement.

Hettie had a sudden acute awareness of the glass that divided them from Starr. Here she was sharing such closeness with one man while another man—her lover—was just inches away. The conflict tore at her and she felt a wild urge to smash the glass between them in an attempt to make an impact on him. To show him just what she thought of his emotional and physical barriers. She almost hated him for throwing her into the path of temptation with Darryl and for a second she wanted to punish him. To really give him something to be jealous about!

But before she could succumb to her irrational urges, Darryl suddenly began to rub his eyes more vigorously and grimace.

"Is the headache worse?" she inquired, flooded with guilt and shame at what she'd nearly done. "Is there anything I can do?"

"It's all right." Darryl smiled but it was clearly a manufactured one. "But I think I ought to take one of my tablets—" Reaching into the pocket of his tight jeans, he drew out a blister pack of pills. "I'll need some water though."

Hettie reached into the luxurious car's small cocktail cabinet and brought out a bottle of mineral water. When Darryl popped a tablet into his mouth, she handed it to him and he drank down the cool water, his throat rippling as he swallowed.

"Would you think I'm an awfully bad guest if I tried to go to sleep again for a while? This medicine generally works better if I have a nap."

"Of course, you're not a bad guest," she said with a soft laugh. "You have a sleep. I'm sure you'll feel better for it."

As she watched, Darryl lay back against the upholstery and almost immediately, his long dark lashes fluttered down. Within a moment or two, it was obvious he was fast asleep.

Now that's both of them who are keeping their distances. Hettie sighed as her companion's breathing grew deep and steady.

And yet she felt no irritation with him, just an intense relief. A great burden of temptation had just been lifted from her.

Am I dreaming? I think I must be... Per Dio, please don't let me wake up!

Darryl's heart began to race as Hettie leaned gracefully towards him for a kiss, and in the split second before her lips met his, his cock leapt to full, throbbing hardness.

LESSONS & LOVERS

Her fingertips traveled over his body beneath his T-shirt, and he gasped as her thumbs flicked lightly at his nipples. This was the sort of thing that men did to women but it was wonderful that it pleasured his male body too. What would it feel like if she did it while his cock was inside her?

Carefully, tentatively, he began to repay the compliment, tugging at her silky black top. His fingers shook, but the silk came out easily and seemed to puff away from her skin it was so light.

Hettie's breasts were exquisite when he lifted his hands to caress them, the curves firm and resilient, the nipples like small stones that bored into his palms. He squeezed and she matched his groan with one of her own, arching her back so she could push herself forward.

She wriggled wildly in his hold, and he felt her fingers scrabbling at his body, nails digging into his rib cage as a giant shudder went through her. For a second he thought he'd hurt her, but she was still gasping with obvious pleasure. Her beautiful face twisted as she arched and threw back her head. He didn't have to be told she was climaxing.

His cock was burning now, stiff in his shorts like a bar of superheated iron. Any suffering he'd felt a moment ago was forgotten, swamped by a greater suffering that was also glorious and welcome. His whole body seemed to ache for her and he felt a powerful urge to double up around the engorged agony in his penis.

Emerging from her own pleasure, and clearly sensing his need, Hettie reached for the hem of her waterfall skirt and drew it up slowly and elegantly.

Beneath she wore tiny black panties, a high-cut wisp of lace that barely covered her pussy and seemed ruder somehow than if she'd been completely naked. The leg line swooped up to her waist and as she shifted her weight to flip her skirt from beneath her, he saw the whole of one sleek white buttock. Placing her hands on either side of her slender hips she slid her brief panties down her thighs.

Darryl felt like a frozen dummy, unable to move. He groaned when she edged forward on the seat, opened her thighs even wider and reached in to tease apart the lips of her sex with her fingers.

And even when she took her fingertips away, her body still pouted at him. His hand felt limp in hers as she took it and drew it to her.

She was like damp silk to his touch, and feeling dazed he let his fingers rest where she'd laid them. He was touching the most sensitive and precious part of her and he had to force himself to breathe.

Controlling his trembling, Darryl let his fingertips skate over her, exploring the folds first then pushing one finger into her pussy. She whimpered softly when he pushed a little harder, and with a clever feline little swivel, seemed to screw herself down on his digit and get it even deeper inside her. The passage was easy, very easy, because she was very wet.

With a gasp of pleasure, Hettie tossed her head from side to side and Darryl knew that he'd got her. That he'd touched her how she wanted to be touched. Needed to be touched. He swirled his thumb and she crooned in response, undulating in that oh-so-telling way as her hot flesh grabbed at his finger in orgasm.

When her body finally stilled, she wriggled slightly and disengaged herself from his fingers, her eyes fluttering open as she did so. Her pupils looked hazy and dilated, but she seemed to sharpen up and take notice as her gaze panned slowly down his body. Following her eyes, Darryl saw to his amazement that his free hand was clamped at the apex of his thighs.

As his heart revved up to treble time, Darryl watched

entranced as Hettie's slender fingers went to work on his belt and the zipper on his jeans. Quickly and deftly, she began to work his jeans down over his hips and thighs, giving him an "up!" to make him lift bottom from the seat and let the tight denim slide on its way.

He felt faint and helpless as she bunched her voluminous skirts in her left hand and threw one long milky thigh across both of his. It was like watching an erotic ballet, and he saw Hettie's thighs tense as she held herself above him for a moment while she reached down and took hold of the head of his cock.

Her touch felt like swansdown as she lowered her sex slowly onto him, feeding him delicately into her moist heat as she descended.

Darryl felt like screaming, weeping and throwing himself bodily up into the air to get deeper inside her.

He was enclosed in a liquid sweetness that seemed to ripple and grip and caress him. It was nothing like masturbation and nothing like he'd expected. He was in two kinds of paradise at once, floating on a cloud and sliding down, down, down into the deepest well of exquisite drowning sensation. He knew he could last only seconds. It was too good, too intense, too much—he could already feel his spine dissolving and a great white ball of pleasure going critical in the pit of his loins.

As Hettie began to bounce on him, he saw her grimace slightly and heard her make a long low indecipherable sound of satisfaction. Settling into a quick deep rhythm, she put her hands down to the juncture of their bodies and Darryl watched in wonder as she flicked her own clitoris in time to their bumps and grinds. He wanted to do it for her, or to hold her breasts again, but suddenly she was moving too furiously and he seemed to have no strength in any part of his body but his cock.

Then suddenly the world dwindled to a minute black point

that exploded out again to every part of him at once. His balls jerked and his semen came scalding up out of them. Shooting out of his sex into hers.

"Oh, yes! Yes! Yes!" he murmured, the words growing faint as pleasure obliterated him and the magic world of his dream drifted away into slumberous darkness.

Chapter Six

Should I have said something? Hettie asked herself, finding it hard to stop herself from grinning as she put clothing into the top drawer of her mahogany dresser.

Watching Darryl sleep had been a revelatory experience. His erotic writhing had left her in no doubt that he'd dreamed about sex. And in her sensitized state it had been an irresistible turn-on. She'd found herself gripping her own crotch as he'd gripped his, and it had been difficult to keep herself from crying out as she'd worked herself to a quick, light orgasm. But she'd remained silent. To wake him would have embarrassed him profoundly.

As it was, he hadn't woken and after coming to the inevitable conclusion of his wet dream, he'd seemed to drift into an even deeper level of slumber. And when he did wake, he hadn't shown the slightest hint that he was aware of what had happened.

Starr too had shown no signs of emotion when the extended car journey was over, and had simply regarded his passengers with his usual inscrutable politeness.

No change there, then.

Hettie had frowned and her eyes had followed his tall,

dark-clad form as he'd set about disposing of their luggage and going about all the usual jobs involved in opening up the beautiful country house. She would have given anything to be able to read the thoughts contained in that strong, close-cropped head of his.

Dragonwood had been partially closed since Piers' death and with the regular staff on extended paid leave, Starr had arranged for a couple from the nearby village to come in for a few hours each morning and do a few basic housekeeping jobs.

Hettie was grateful for this and was rather looking forward to them fending for themselves around the house. Doing things like sneaking down to the kitchen for a sandwich whenever she felt hungry, making her own bed, taking morning cups of tea to Darryl and Stevie. If Starr would let her do any of that, of course. She was the "Lady of the Manor" in his eyes, and must not be seen to be roughing it!

She'd also been hoping that Starr would assign himself a room near hers, but no such luck. He'd taken his usual room—in the staff wing—which would be a good two-hundred-yard tiptoe away in the dark! As it was, Hettie had Darryl on one side and Stevie, when she arrived, on the other.

Still naked after she'd washed the dust of travel and the stickiness of masturbation from her body, Hettie went on unpacking with only half her mind really on the task.

Darryl had looked so sensual! Watching him bring himself off could get to be a dangerously distracting habit. It would be far too easy to indulge in such delicious, self-indulgent voyeurism—and avoid facing the major issue that troubled her.

Starr.

She sighed. It would probably have been a better idea

to take herself off to a chaste, monastic retreat somewhere and think things through rather than come down here and immerse herself in hedonism.

She took a black wet-look bikini out of her case and wriggled into it. The suit was minuscule and clinging, and she might as well have been nude, as Stevie had suggested. Hettie frowned in front of the mirror for a few minutes, but no amount of tugging and adjusting could make the suit look any less indecent. And unfortunately, she had no other swimwear that was any less revealing.

But does it matter? She grimaced at her reflection.

It won't make the slightest bit of difference to the way Starr behaves if I really do *parade around naked. And I'm sure Darryl would still fancy me if I wore a feed sack!*

Shaking her head, she slid her body into a thin black wrap and her feet into flat sandals. Grabbing a bottle of sunblock and a towel, she left her clothes half unpacked and made her way down the stairs and along the length of the main hall.

She felt an intense longing to take the bull by the horns, and to find Starr and confront him. Speak her mind and her heart while the urge was upon her and before she could lose her courage—but neither the kitchen nor any of the utility rooms revealed him. And when she backtracked towards his quarters and knocked on the door, there was no answer there either. He was most probably working somewhere else around the house, or in the garden. Or maybe he'd even gone into the local village for additional provisions. But wherever he was, it *felt* as if her tall, blond servant had simply vanished off the face of the Earth!

"Screw you, then!" she muttered. Her sandals flapping angrily against the tiled floor, she strode through the house, heading for the terrace, where they were supposed to be having lunch. That was if the elusive Starr had made the preparations before he'd gone his own sweet way.

The terrace was an inviting stone-flagged area that hugged one side of the house and was flanked by a broad flat-topped parapet. A set of shallow stone steps led down towards the swimming pool and the tiered and landscaped gardens beyond, and a trellised canopy at the far end provided a welcome area of shade on sunny days.

Some instinct or premonition made her pause on the path by the garden wall. She stopped and slid off her sandals, then clutched them in her hand with her sunblock and her towel. Moving barefoot on the narrow grass border that ran beside the gravel path, she padded along stealthily, managing to reach the stone-flagged terrace without disturbing its single, sun-worshipping occupant.

In the open, unshaded portion of the terrace, Darryl was stretched out on a lounge chair. He was naked, but for a skimpy pair of black bathing trunks and virtually motionless. He'd clearly not spent as much time dithering in his room as Hettie had because his lean bronzed back was shiny with sunblock and his steady, even breathing suggested he'd already fallen asleep. Silently putting down her belongings, Hettie moved as close she dared risk without waking him.

Standing like a statue, she had an intensely female urge to stroke his glistening shoulders, and simply worship his youth and his sun-graced perfection. He was male and he was beautiful. And he was *here*, in front of her. Unlike that other glorious man who kept making her so angry and confused.

But before she could do anything rash, Darryl stirred, then tensed and suddenly turned over.

"Oh, I'm so sorry!" he gasped, sitting up. "I didn't mean to fall asleep. It's just that the sun felt so good on my skin and it made me feel drowsy." Swiftly, he reached for his towel and flung it across his hips—but not before Hettie was treated to an eyeful of a magnificent stiffening hard-on straining at the shiny fabric of his trunks. Looking swiftly away, she felt her blood surge in her veins as if fired by lightning.

"Come on let's sit in the shade for a bit," she said quickly. "It's better for me, and I could do with a glass of something." She nodded towards the seating area and the rustic table spread out with buffet food set over chill packs, and to the bottles that stood cooling in a stainless steel ice bucket. Clearly the ever-efficient Starr had already been here and prepared the lunch, although God alone knew how he'd managed so much in so little a space of time.

Darryl was quite pink-faced when he followed her into the shade, a pair of baggy, multicolored surf shorts now preserving his modesty. "I really am sorry," he apologized again, biting his lip, a picture of horny bashfulness. "I didn't mean for that to happen. I hope I haven't embarrassed you."

"Don't worry. No problem," said Hettie, attempting to sound unperturbed but knowing she wasn't doing a very good job of it. The afterimage of his perfect male body so obviously aroused was doing wicked things to her nervous system. "You've got a wonderful body, you shouldn't be ashamed of it," she went on lightly. "Now... do you want water, or wine or fruit juice? We seem to have everything here, thanks to Starr."

Darryl requested water and she handed him a bottle, then poured a glass of wine for herself. She wasn't much of a drinker, but right now she needed it.

The wine tasted dry and light but its crisp, almost sharp tang couldn't cut through her thoughts and distract her from them.

What the hell is wrong with me? I think I'm in love with Starr and yet here I am with Darryl and I find him attractive too. How can I be like this? It just doesn't make sense.

Things would be so much more clear-cut if I could force myself to speak to Starr. Make him listen. And make him answer me and tell me what he's *feeling... Rather than the two of us continuing to dance around each other in this nonspeaking, all-fucking puppet show!*

Recklessly, Hettie drained the whole glass at once, and as she reached out for a refill she nodded that Darryl should drink his water.

As he raised the water to his lips, his gorgeous mouth suddenly captivated her, and to her acute consternation, she found herself imagining what it would be like to kiss it.

Stop it! She glowered at the bottle of Frascati she'd just picked up and put it back in the cooler. *Enough already, or you'll do something you might regret,*

But when Darryl put down his bottle, his face suddenly paled beneath the gold of his tan. He stared at the wine bottle in the cooler with a look pure shock on his face.

"*Frascati*," he said, the words barely more than a whisper.

Why would the name of the wine bother him? Hettie glanced at the bottle too, but there was nothing unusual about it.

"Yes. It's very nice," she said, at a loss. "Would you like to try a taste?"

"I've drunk that wine before," Darryl murmured, almost as if he hadn't heard her.

She looked at him closely. Beneath his tan, his face was pinched and taut. Was something coming back to him?

"At Renata's?"

"No! Before!" Like an automaton, he moved closer, picked up the bottle and tried to refill Hettie's glass. But he was shaking so much that the golden wine spilled all over her hand.

Hettie took the bottle from him and mopped up the mess

with a towel. Then she guided Darryl to one of the garden couches and hunkered down beside him.

"What is it, Darryl?" She put an arm around his bare shoulder.

"We had Frascati. We used to sit at this old wooden table and eat pasta and drink a glass of wine together. All day out in the sun... Or digging...somewhere... We'd be tired by suppertime...but so happy. Full of a sense of achievement." His handsome face crumpled suddenly and to Hettie's horror, she realized he was fighting tears. "Oh Hettie, I miss him so!" Moved by his plight, she hugged him closer.

He'd obviously remembered his adoptive uncle. And from the depth of his anguish it was also obvious that Darryl was now aware that his beloved relative—his father figure—was dead.

Hettie felt tears well in her own eyes.

Oh Piers!

Suddenly an immense bolt of loss stabbed at her heart. It was the same. It hurt so much. The pain of knowing that the most important person in your life was gone forever. That was the pain that Darryl was feeling right now—the same pain she'd felt when the doctor had pronounced Piers finally at peace.

As she held the grieving Darryl, Hettie suddenly wondered again where Starr was. *He* was the one who'd been there when *she'd* needed a pair of arms around her. Without him, she would have fallen apart she'd been so lost and alone.

Confused urges jostled her. Unconsciously, she began to rock Darryl in her arms, just the way she would have done with anyone who was suffering. And yet at the same time she was acutely aware of his intense masculinity. The heat of his skin. The strong musculature of his lean but well-shaped limbs. The perilous proximity of that splendid cock she'd been unable to tear her eyes away from just a few moments ago.

Darryl smelled good. He felt good. She couldn't imagine it *not* being good to make love to him and have him make love to her. And she knew from personal experience the healing and restorative powers of good sex.

She was trembling. In another world, she might have welcomed this beautiful man into her body to help heal his sadness.

But of course she couldn't. This was the real world, and to sleep with Darryl was beyond unthinkable. Because of her own memories of being comforted the same way while Piers was ill. She couldn't do it because of the man who'd comforted her then.

She patted Darryl's sleek back, aware of the perfection of his skin but also imagining the touch of another man's skin and the intense, burning blue of his eyes as she seemed to watch her.

A soft cough made Hettie jump and she jerked back from an equally surprised Darryl, expecting to find that man— and those blue eyes—to be right there on the patio *really* watching her.

"Is everything all right?" inquired Stevie. Her voice was gentle and professional, in spite of the fact she was wearing a skimpy olive green T-shirt, a floppy hat and a pair of voluminous ex-army shorts.

Hettie was more relieved than she cared to admit to see her friend right at that moment and flashed Stevie a welcoming smile. She expected Darryl to be awkward, having been caught in tears by an unknown woman, but quite the reverse. Composed and graceful, he rose to his feet, rubbed quickly at his eyes then held out his hand towards Stevie.

"Hello, you must be Dr. Madrigan. I'm Darryl di Angeli.

How do you do?"

"*Ciao. Piacere,*" replied Stevie with a grin. Hettie could see that even though her friend's smile was warm and friendly, the doctor was astutely sizing up the situation as a clinician and assessing Darryl and his emotions.

A stream of musical Italian issued from Darryl's lips, but Stevie only laughed and shrugged. "I'm afraid that's about the extent of my knowledge of your language, Darryl," she said, taking his hand and shaking it. "And yes I am Stephanie Madrigan, but you can call me Stevie." She glanced over Darryl's shoulder and winked. "Any more of that wine left, Hett? I'm dying of thirst here!"

"Lots. Let me get you a glass," said Hettie, rising to her feet and bustling around to get Stevie some wine.

She felt a great glow of gratitude. The older woman had arrived and immediately taken control of the situation with tact and delicacy. Behind her, Hettie could hear her two companions chatting easily about the beautiful weather and the equally beautiful gardens. They were classic British topics of conversation—but always wonderfully comforting when you were making a brand-new friend.

As the sun beat down, the three of them continued to sit in the shade and talk. It was mostly Stevie who led the conversation, and Hettie smiled to herself as she admired the way her friend was able to draw Darryl out and ask him gentle questions about himself without seeming to be in the slightest bit intrusive or prying.

Years of practice, I suppose. She caught Stevie's eye for a split second and saw her nod in acknowledgement. For all her eccentricities and her sexual forthrightness, the doctor was eminent and respected in her profession.

Maybe I should turn you loose on Starr, Stevie, Hettie said silently to her friend. *I'm getting nowhere trying to break down his wall... Maybe you can do it?*

But even as she thought the thought, Hettie knew it was unlikely. Starr was private and impenetrable, locked behind barriers of his own making. He'd give his body unstintingly but never a hint of what was happening in his heart.

The afternoon wore on. Peacefully and amenably. Despite her frustration over Starr, Hettie's heart warmed to see Darryl so relaxed and at ease with Stevie. And she grinned to herself at his obvious sexual interest in the good doctor.

"It's just too hot!" said Stevie suddenly, standing up beside her lounger, her hands on the hem of her shirt. "Does anybody mind?" she queried, but before either Hettie or Darryl could speak, she'd whipped off the thin garment and bared her small but shapely breasts to the afternoon heat. Her shorts and the miniscule thong she'd been wearing beneath them quickly followed.

Hettie hardly dared look at Darryl, but as she watched Stevie begin to smooth sunblock over her slender, athletic body, she felt a *frisson* of reaction in her own flesh.

She's beautiful. And if I wanted to go that way, I know she and I could be together.

It was a piquant fantasy, and for a moment Hettie imagined describing it to the one she really wanted to be with. Where the hell was he? Had he come back from wherever he'd disappeared to yet?

"How about doing my back, Darryl?" said Stevie, lowering herself onto a lounge chair, on her front. Then, looking seductively back over her shoulder, she held out the tube of sunblock to the young Italian. The air was suddenly heavy and charged, and as Hettie watched a play of emotion dance across Darryl's smooth face, she realized that it was far more than a chance to apply the lotion that Stevie was offering him.

Oh Lord, this is it! She hid a smile behind her fingers. *Stevie said she'd come down here to help with his "education"…and the first lesson is about to start now!*

Time to make herself scarce.

"Er—yes—of course," replied Darryl, getting up. His voice sounded a little odd, but in a distinctly excited way. His eyes were dark, the pupils hugely dilated and as she watched him take the tube from Stevie's fingers, Hettie swiftly gathered up her belongings and shrugged into her wrap. Her friend the doctor was looking at the young man with a very direct, inviting smile upon her face. And Hettie guessed that Darryl wouldn't even notice if somebody dropped a piano into the pool right now, much less take much notice of her own exit from the scene.

"It's too hot for me out here now," she said, already walking away and not giving anybody time for false protests that she should stay. "I'm going in for a shower. I'll see the two of you later."

Casting one last glimpse at the couple on the patio, she saw Darryl flash her a smile that was both surprised, and at the same time strangely complicit…and grateful. And as he turned his attention back to Stevie, the doctor winked knowingly at Hettie.

And now for you, Mr. Starr!

Her face set and determined, Hettie swept through the house, her thin wrap flying behind her. She didn't really know where to start looking. He hadn't been in the kitchen, the pantry or his own room last time she'd searched for him, but that didn't mean he couldn't be in any one of those places now. The man was so elusive he could be just about anywhere.

But she was damned well going to find him if it killed her!

Finding herself hovering outside his room, she studied the wooden door as if it might tell her whether he was beyond it.

Strange quivers rippled through her. It was sex, she realized, her mind flicking to what might be happening on the patio between Stevie and Darryl. But it was so much more than that. She *had* to fathom Starr, to know him. Having acknowledged her love for him, the situation that existed between them was no longer enough for her. She had to get close to him in a way that he'd never, ever allowed her to. She wanted more, and somehow she had to make him decide whether he wanted more too.

Or whether the whole thing had to end.

The sound of her knock on the door seemed astonishingly loud, but it brought no answer. Hettie's heart pounded. She couldn't be thwarted now, she just couldn't.

Again, she pounded on the door. Again nothing. Not giving herself time to think she tried the handle, turned it and found that the room wasn't locked.

Heart fluttering and leaping, she stepped into the somber, tidy, almost ascetic room. She knew that Starr had always been offered every home comfort for his accommodations, but his bedroom still had the spare, uncluttered feeling of a monk's cell.

"Some monk!" she growled to herself, moving inside and glancing around. Barely any possessions sullied the stark orderliness of the room's surfaces. On the bedside cabinet there stood a small, cheap-looking alarm clock, a bottle of water and a paperback book. A military biography she discovered when she picked it up and flipped to the page marked by a simple black leather bookmark.

Crossing to the chest of drawers, she picked up the items that were set upon it. An unlabeled bottle that on opening revealed Starr's subtle but strangely exciting cologne. A pair of cuff links. A plain black clothesbrush.

The only other items on show in the room were an art magazine neatly placed on the ottoman at the foot of the bed and an inexpensive portfolio from a discount stationery house set beside it.

Starr's drawings.

Hettie's fingers twitched with a desire to open up the portfolio and look inside. Having studied and worked in art, her curiosity about his work was almost as ferocious as her hunger to know the mysteries of his heart. In fact the one might be the window to the other. But no amount of requests to view his drawings had ever induced him to show them to her. He was like iron, and completely unmovable on the issue. It was the one thing that they'd almost but not quite actually argued about.

She ran her fingers over the cardboard surface of the portfolio. The evidence of Starr's secret talent was just the merest flick of her fingers away—but suddenly Hettie knew she mustn't reveal it. She was already invading his privacy unforgivably, but in this one thing she could still respect his boundaries.

Abandoning the portfolio, she turned and saw a single black cotton shirt on a hanger hooked to the front of an old-fashioned mahogany wardrobe.

Unable to control herself, Hettie plucked the shirt from the hanger and pressed it to her face. It'd been worn, and not only was it scented with the same cologne from the bottle, but there was also a fainter, more insidious, more blood-stirring fragrance. The fresh, yet disturbingly musky scent of Starr's warm skin…

Pressing her mouth and nose against the thin black cloth, Hettie felt her loins kick hard and surge for its wearer.

Oh, Starr! She inhaled his essence and longed, longed, longed for the feeling of his hard flesh inside her. She had never wanted him more than at this moment. The craving was so intense that her knees trembled and she swayed on her feet. Stepping shakily, she backed up until she found herself at Starr's narrow, neatly made bed.

Collapsing backwards, she lay down still clutching the black shirt, with its evocative odor, to her face.

Each breath seemed to make him more real to her. Each breath made the need for him ache and ache and ache. Unconsciously, she rubbed her thighs together to try and ease the torment. With a shock, she realized what she was doing and slid her hand down to her crotch and pressed her fingers hard against her pussy through the skimpy black wisp of her bikini bottom.

Closing her eyes tightly, she sank into a world of scent and sensation. The scent of Starr. The pressure of not her fingers but his, working with increasing fervor against her clitoris. Orgasm barreled quickly towards her, rising from the depths of her love for him and blooming in a sad, deep sweetness beneath her pounding fingertips.

"Oh Starr! Oh Starr!" she groaned, her pussy clutching at emptiness, clutching at the void where he should be.

For a while, she just lay there clutching the shirt, astonished and very scared by the tears that had trickled from beneath her tightly closed eyelids. Crying for Starr? What was to become of her? It wasn't all that long since she'd lost the husband she'd been devoted to and yet here she was weeping for another man…

A long, firm and very familiar tread on the landing brought her shooting to her feet and she flung the black shirt willy-nilly across the bed. The door opened and she froze like some tiny, terrified prey animal before an unstoppable predator.

"Milady?"

A frown momentarily pleated Starr's broad, tanned brow. He stepped across the threshold, his movements relaxed and economical as ever. But in spite of her own confusion, Hettie could see he was clearly shocked to find her in his room.

But a second later, his familiar, glasslike mask was back in place and his voice was a smooth and even as it always was.

"I'm sorry, was there something you wanted?"

Chapter Seven

Yes! You! You're what I want! Hettie was dumbstruck anew by the beauty of the secretive blond paragon who served her.

Starr had been running or jogging or exercising somehow, because he wore only shorts and an abbreviated athletic shirt and a battered old pair of well-worn running shoes. His gilded arms gleamed with perspiration and there was a ruddy glow of exertion across his face, throat and chest.

If Hettie had been hungry for him before, she was ravenous now—especially with her senses piqued by thoughts of what Stevie and Darryl might be doing.

In an uncharacteristically unstudied gesture, Starr lifted an arm and rubbed the back of his hand across his sweat-streaked brow, making Hettie shiver with lust at the strangely vulnerable sight of a tuft of golden hair in his armpit. She wanted to rub her face in that hot niche and absorb his earthy smell and taste, then smear the spoor of his dominant maleness across her cheeks.

"Milady?" he queried softly again, wiping his hand down his shorts. His blue eyes were still wary. Hettie had never been to this room before and she wondered if her presence here fazed him.

"Er...no, not really... I just wondered where you were," she said, glancing at the shirt on the bed and wondering if he'd remember that he'd left it hanging up.

Of course he'll remember! He's Starr and he's never been known to forget or overlook anything!

"I've been for a run, milady," he said, lifting his hands again and this time passing both across his closely cropped scalp, "But if there's anything you require, I can be showered in a few moments. Perhaps a cold drink? Or afternoon tea? Just give me five minutes."

He did nothing other than rub sweat from his face and neck, but Hettie could read the unspoken agenda. He wanted her out of his room and back within the normal parameters of their relationship. His bedroom was "staff" and she was the lady of the house. She was out of place here.

"Look!" she said suddenly, taking the brakes off, sick and tired of divisions and parameters. "You don't have to skulk around in here or in the kitchen or go for runs and disappear all the time. Why don't you join us, out on the terrace? Just hang out for a while. You're not just a servant, Starr. You're much, much more than that. And you always have been. Surely you know that?"

It was as if shutter came down across his face, closing out any hint of the emotion she'd seen a few moments ago.

"My place is to take care of your welfare and your household, ma'am," he said expressionlessly. "It's inappropriate for me to expect to socialize with you and your guests."

Hettie curled her hands into fists, furiously angry. He was so goddamned stubborn! So determined to stick to the rigid role he'd assigned himself.

How could she ever get through to him? Force her way

through his façade? The words *I love you, you stubborn bastard!* rose to her lips but she couldn't utter them. Not in the face of that cool, glacial expression.

She decided to try another tack.

"Darryl fancies me, you know!" she cried, throwing back her head, bringing her chin up defiantly. "Aren't you afraid that if you leave us alone together too much, he'll make a pass at me? And I'll respond. Because you're not there? I bet he wouldn't just retreat behind some kind of cold, emotionless wall when he'd made love to me… With him, it'd be warm. Close. Normal."

She watched for signs. Something… Anything… But nothing happened. "Aren't you jealous? Don't you think I'm a slut? Thinking about having sex with a man I've only just met?"

Not a flicker. If anything the cool lines of his face grew harder than ever.

"My job isn't to judge you or question you, milady, simply to be here for you when you need me."

Dear God, he could have been discussing the weather! Hettie took a step towards him, every muscle in her body taut. She'd always thought the expression "her blood boiled" was just a cliché, but she could almost feel it happening to her now. Frustrated anger bubbled and welled up in her like molten lava. Seeking release…

"Then be here for me now!" she hissed, locking her eyes with his as she fought to get a reaction, "I want *you*. *Now*. Not some other man… And don't call me 'milady'! I'm Hettie! You fuck me, remember?"

His face was still as smooth as glass, yet opaque. Giving nothing…and yet…and yet, was that a flash of something? An instantly suppressed flare of furious emotion?

And it was that act of suppression that made Hettie snap.

Before she could think or reason, she whipped back her arm and backhanded him right across the face with her entire strength.

There was a long, drawn out moment. Tension thickened between them as Starr's golden face turned pink where she'd struck him. Then, moving with catlike, preternatural speed, he enveloped her savagely in his arms, crushing her mouth beneath his as he ground an erection like iron into her belly.

Hettie's knees felt like paper, her bones dissolving. This was what she'd wanted so long, so very long. Longer, she realized faintly as her mouth was punished and possessed, than she and Starr had ever had any kind of relationship.

This… This *real* emotion, she suddenly understood in both horror and wonder, was what she'd wanted since the first evening Piers had taken her home from the art gallery, and introduced her to the tall, grave man who drove his limousine. This beautiful man had been bone deep in her senses even while she'd fallen in love with his employer.

Moaning, she yielded all her mouth to him and helplessly rubbed her body against him, abrading her swollen nipples against his hard chest and massaging his amazing hard-on shamelessly with her belly.

He was so big. So hot. The heat burned through their insubstantial clothing and brought fresh saliva to Hettie's plundered mouth. With a yearning so intense it made her groan, she wanted one of the few sexual acts that Starr had always denied her. The one he would not allow because he'd devoted himself to her pleasure alone and not his.

She wanted to taste him. Feel his magnificence fill her mouth and invade it—subdue her with its size and force. Shaking herself free, she sank to her knees and plucked at the waistband of his shorts, fighting to free him in readiness for her attentions.

But as fast as before, Starr took control, grasping her hands and holding her away from him. He glared down at her, blue eyes on fire as never before.

"No!" he said, through his gritted white teeth.

Why not?

Hettie was struck dumb and unable to act by the shock of this new, ferocious Starr. Totally limp, she allowed him to lift her, almost throw her across the narrow Spartan bed and strip away the flimsy bottoms of her bikini. Opening her thighs, she finally gained a hold of her senses and reached for him. Her sex flexed and fluttered, almost convulsing already at the thought of having him in her.

But Starr shocked her again. With a sudden animal grace, he sank to his knees between her spread thighs, pressing them even further apart with his long, golden hands.

"Oh no!" cried Hettie, comprehending instantly what he was about to do.

No! He was going to use his marvelous mouth on her to distract her. Divert her from her course and silence her questions and her desire for the truth. And with his face between her thighs, he could hide his eyes and whatever emotion they contained from her searching gaze.

"No!" she insisted again. "This isn't my choice! I want to—"

Starr lifted his face for just a moment and his steely regard silenced her. His sensuous mouth was a thin, determined line. A slash of real anger. Of command.

"I can and I will," he said, the controlled voice at odds with the blazing eyes. "This— This is *my* choice!"

Then, leaning forward, he buried his face between her thighs.

Hettie let out a high keening cry, almost jackknifing up off the bed as Starr went straight for her clitoris, sucking hard on the tiny nub of flesh to extract the maximum response in the minimum amount of time. An almost painful spasm wrenched at her sex, sending her into thrashing paroxysms of mindless pleasure, all thought of Darryl, of Piers, of the existence of any other man on the face of the earth totally banished.

She was still coming, still squirming and struggling, when Starr changed his tack and began to lap and lave at her entire pussy. His long warm tongue swept over her folds, stroking up and down from her clitoris to her anus, before diving inside her. Furled, it was as solid and potent as a cock and fucked her just as hard. Hettie shouted incoherently, coming again and rising to a new height of sensation that was almost overwhelming.

A moment later, he swirled his tongue again and went back to licking wickedly at the very nexus of her pleasure, and the levels ramped up to a pitch that she simply couldn't cope with…

Still moaning his name, she gave up trying and all went black.

Hettie!

Starr's cry was as silent as it was agonized. Almost staggering to his feet, he stared down at her—the object of his adoration spread out and vulnerable before him on his own bed.

He pressed a hand to his mouth. To the taste of her there, the most sublime nectar, the taste of life. Turbulent emotions roiled in him, twisting his gut and his heart. For a moment he imagined her with Darryl as she'd described, and he almost wanted to die from the excruciating pain of it!

He loved her with all his heart, yet he could never claim *her* love for himself.

She still loved her husband.

She was rare, special and precious and he was nothing.

Well, not nothing, but someone who had escaped from a life at the bottom of the pond of crime and corruption by just the skin of his teeth. And through the gracious kindness of a man he would never, ever have been able to repay, even if he still lived.

Hettie, for all her natural friendliness and her unaffected ways, was an aristocratic woman who had married an aristocratic man. Starr had come from the gutter, dragged up barely knowing the parents who couldn't have given damn about him and to whom stealing and worse were normal, everyday activities. The difference between his background and that of the exquisite woman sprawled before him should not have mattered in a modern egalitarian society. But it did to him. And he could never ever tell her...

But suddenly, as he looked down on her, a realization out of nowhere almost unmanned him. It was like a kick in the gut and he actually gasped.

You're a coward, man, aren't you? A stupid coward. You hide behind the class thing. Behind duty... Behind Piers Miller... Because you're afraid that she'll reject you if you tell her how you really feel.

He closed his eyes for a second, a strong grown man, erect and dominant. Yet at the same time he felt the reeling uncertainty of adolescence and first love, and the fear of being found wanting by the object of his adoration.

But still he ached like the very devil for her. His cock was like iron, a heavy, dragging bar of torment. And her splayed legs invited him to plunge between them and assuage the pain of a need that threatened to bend him double. She was there in front of him, her moist pink sex pouting and open. How simple it would be just to tear off his shorts and plunge his burning rod into her. He'd be finished in moments, so intensely did he want her. And with his strength, and her relative fragility, there was no way on earth she could stop him.

Do it! Have her! Fuck her! some inner demon raged at him. It even drove him to slip down his shorts and cradle his trigger-happy cock.

But he couldn't. To take his beloved now would be to betray everything he felt about her. Every trust that both she and her dead husband had put in him. He bit his lower lip, holding in his heartfelt moan of need and love.

Somehow though, he must have release and he must have it with her. Staring down at the crimson gleam of her exposed pussy, he narrowed his eyes. So wet. Wet with his saliva and with her satin lubrication. Somehow he had to join with her, to blend himself with her. Make the two of them one without descending to the baseness of possessing her unconscious body...

"Oh Hettie, I love you" he whispered, transfixed by her and ensorcelled by her. Slowly at first, then quickly, he began to pump his penis with his hand, gritting his teeth at the pleasure-pain. Then, he ravaged his lip again as the sensations soared and his come powered up as if from the very depths of his soul and jetted in tribute towards his lady.

Tasting blood in his mouth and bittersweet ecstasy in his cock, he watched his pearly seed splash against the beautiful folds of his beloved's perfect sex.

What happened? What did he do to me? Did he touch me?

The questions rolled over and over in Hettie's brain as she pressed the soft, fluffy towel between her legs and patted herself dry. She'd been asking them ever since she'd woken up alone and lying on her own bed—when the last thing she'd remembered was passing out from pleasure while Starr was giving her head.

He must have carried me back here.

She looked around the bathroom, thinking of her awakening in the room beyond. A light day blanket had been tenderly draped across her, and on the bedside table, someone—Starr, obviously—had left a tall glass of chilled, homemade lemonade and a plate of grapes, cherries and other fruit neatly sliced and arranged.

I don't deserve him. She blotted her welling eyes quickly before applying some moisturizer. *I make demands. I shout at him. I throw a tantrum because I want more than duty allows him to give. And still he cherishes me and treats me like a princess.* Even the bath she'd just enjoyed had been drawn and scented with her favorite fragrance ready for her.

If only I could remember what happened!

Did he fuck me? She asked the question, but knew the answer. Starr had been hard as iron, primed and ready, but no way would he have just taken her like that. It just wasn't in his nature. It would violate his code of behavior and everything he stood for.

And yet... She'd felt so sticky and slick between her legs. And when she'd tentatively put a finger to her crotch then tasted it, she could almost have imagined it was semen.

But it couldn't be. It couldn't be.

"About time!" said a familiar voice as Hettie strolled through to her bedroom, wrapped in the big bath towel.

"Stevie!"

The good doctor was reclining elegantly on Hettie's bed, looking as quirkily stylish as ever in a pair of white cricket trousers and a matching white cotton shirt that looked superb over her unfettered breasts.

"You were in the bathroom a long time," Stevie observed, her eyes twinkling. Levering herself to a sitting position, she tossed aside the magazine she'd been reading. "I'm surprised that you need to masturbate after spending time with the admirable Mr. Starr." Her heavily mascara-darkened lashes flicked down and up, just once.

"I wasn't masturbating! And nothing went on with Starr," Hettie lied. "I haven't even seen him since—since before you arrived."

Stevie's fine eyes narrowed. "So what were you doing? Just thinking?"

"Yes."

"What about?"

Hettie walked across to her dressing table and sat down to apply a bit more moisturizer to her face. Concentrating fixedly on her reflection, it was easier to evade Stevie's scrutiny.

"Hettie! What's wrong?" Stevie was behind her now with arms crossed, her gaze locking with Hettie's in the mirror.

Hettie screwed the top on her lotion bottle, then reached for a comb to detangle her damp hair. She could see Stevie was waiting patiently for an answer, but it was difficult to supply one. She didn't really have any answers for herself. She didn't even know what half the questions were.

"I-I was thinking about Starr, who else?"

"Oh Hettie." Stevie's hands were on Hettie's bare shoulders now, slowly massaging. "You mustn't worry... Things have a way of working themselves out. You and Starr are crazy about each other. It's just a matter of time." The doctor's long hands stilled, and she grinned at Hettie in the mirror. "And you needn't worry about looking after Darryl now, either…" Her eyelid drooped in a sly wink.

Hettie found herself relaxing, and she grinned back. She decided not to query the doctor's reference to people "being crazy about each other" but instead she said, "Oh, so you've taken over his education then, have you? Care to tell me what happened between you after I came inside?"

"Oh, just a little hands-on practical work…" Stevie smiled enigmatically. "Role playing…exercises…you know."

Hettie shook her head. "I hardly dare ask." She smiled at her friend in the mirror.

"Darryl's a sweet man," Stevie said more seriously. "I think he's going to be all right." Her gentle fingers worked teasingly on Hettie's shoulders. "And he *really* likes sex. Almost as much as you do."

"So… *Very* hands-on then?" It was Hettie's turn to wink back at Stevie, who looked inordinately pleased with herself.

"Very," the doctor confirmed, with a very cat-who-got-the-cream grin. She glanced towards the dress and underclothes that Hettie had set out on a chair ready to put on. "Put some clothes on that luscious body of yours and stop making me think about sex! It's time for dinner."

Hettie dressed quickly, feeling a little self-conscious, even though Stevie was making a big point of being engrossed in her magazine. She slid into black silk high cut panties and shapely underwire bra, then a matching skimpily styled garter belt and sheer black stockings.

"What're you trying to do? Make all of us come at the dining table? Even Mister Iceman?" Stevie inquired, finally looking up and checking Hettie out. She obviously approved of the short slim-cut shift dress of black velvet, and the sexy, narrow-heeled court shoes that went with it.

"I just want to look nice," Hettie replied pertly, fluffing out her hair a bit more then stepping back to the dressing table to apply makeup. "Just because I'm a widow it doesn't mean I can let myself go to seed!"

"You look wonderful, sweetheart," said Stevie, more softly. "Piers would be very proud of you. Very proud indeed."

"Thanks." Hettie suddenly felt tearful, but fought it down. "I just wish I could be certain that he'd approve of how I feel about Starr. Or how I *think* I feel…" She gestured vaguely, hoping Stevie would understand what she meant. "I'm still not even sure myself. He makes things so difficult!"

"Piers would approve, Hettie. I know it. You know it. He *wanted* you and Starr to get together. He might not have said it overtly to either of you, but it was always his plan. Now, shall we go down and get some dinner? I don't know what you've done to deserve him, you fortunate woman, but that fabulous blond god of yours seems to be a amazing cook on top of everything else!"

Starr had managed an ingenious compromise with their evening meal. In spite of what he'd said earlier, Hettie had still been determined to try and persuade him to eat with them here at Dragonwood. Even if he still insisted on standing on ceremony when they were in London.

Starr's instinctive answer to her dilemma was a barbecue—served on the terrace—which meant he could busy himself cooking, then take his own meal discreetly. Be with them but in his own way still on duty.

Hettie cornered him, standing apart from them, leaning

on the terrace's wide stone parapet sipping a glass of mineral water and looking out intently across the parkland and the roseate sunset beyond.

"Look. About this afternoon. I'm sorry I slapped you," she said quietly. "I shouldn't have done it. It was uncalled for."

It certainly was.

She stared at him. Starr was everything that a strong man should be. Tall, straight and golden, so dramatic in his vestments of darkness. He too, had always worn black since Piers' death. He served her perfectly and what had she done? Taunted him. Insulted him. Slapped him instead of having the courage to sit down and tell him her feelings like a grown-up, civilized woman.

"Think no more about it, ma'am," he replied, for once not meeting her eyes but still staring in the direction of a small woodland copse through which wound a slowly flowing river. "My own behavior was hardly exemplary. It's my place to apologize, not yours. I hope you'll overlook it, and we can forget it ever happened."

"But—"

Starr forestalled her. "Your guests, ma'am," he said, nodding lightly towards where both Stevie and Darryl were peering curiously in their direction.

Hettie took the bull by the horns. "You don't have to do this, you know. Be apart." She so wanted to touch him, to place her hand on his strong, dark-clad arm. But she was intensely aware of the scrutiny of the others. For her part she didn't care that they were looking, but she knew that Starr would hate any "fuss" in front of her guests. "Just because Darryl and Stevie are here, you don't have to be out of the way all the time. I- I—"

How could she put it? She knew she couldn't use the

word "love" right at this moment, because if she did, she would probably lose her composure altogether. And that would cause a scene. For which Starr would blame himself. And that would make matters worse.

But she had to say *something*!

"I want you around, Starr! I want your company. And not just— Oh, I don't know," she blurted out in exasperation, wishing he'd look her in the eye. Longing for him to give her some sign of affection rather than duty.

"I don't want to get in the way, ma'am." His voice was cool and measured.

"But you don't get in the way! How could you possibly get in the way?" she cried angrily, forgetting her resolution of just a moment ago. Her blood was up now and her heart was full of confused emotions. "This thing of ours... Is that all it is to you? A duty? A service you perform? Don't you want me for myself at all?" Across the terrace, Darryl and Stevie were murmuring to each other but Hettie could tell that they were still watching her closely as they sat knee to knee in a pair of garden chairs.

There was a long moment of silence. Hettie felt stunned by her own outburst and numbed to a state of inertia as she leant on the parapet, grateful for its support. The scent of flowers drifted up from the beds below and yet their perfume seemed to be coming from an entirely different world.

At long last Starr answered her, his cool eyes burning suddenly as he turned to her. Blue fire of almost unimaginable heat. "It is my privilege to serve you, milady. My privilege and my joy... More than I can adequately describe." His voice was low and in a rare, revealing moment, reminiscent of the one in his bedroom, Hettie detected a tremor of real emotion.

He does care! Jubilant, she wanted to hug him and

kiss him but knowing he wouldn't welcome it—especially with their companions still watching curiously, their own conversation temporarily forgotten.

Once again, she'd finally broken through to the unflappable, unfazable Starr and the thrill of it gave Hettie back her strength and purpose. He cared for her. He wanted her. Perhaps even loved her. But some bone-deep, archaic streak of chivalry was still preventing him from declaring it. *She* would have to make the moves from now on!

But not right at this moment.

The evening went very smoothly after that considering that everyone—Starr included—was obviously tired. Hardly surprising in Darryl's case, thought Hettie with a grin, enjoying a glass of excellent wine as she eyed Stevie's handsome "pupil".

You and Stevie made love this afternoon, didn't you? Her smile widened and she took another sip of wine to hide it.

It was crystal clear that something had changed with Darryl. There was a twinkle in his eyes all the time, in spite of his occasional yawns, and a new and quite blood-stirring sensuality to his every movement. Put in its simplest terms, when they'd left London this morning he'd still been sexually unsure of himself…and now he knew exactly what he was doing. He'd always had that uncanny sense of poise about him, but now he was flirting with Stevie like an experienced ladies' man and parrying her sexual sophistication with an effortless charm and playfulness.

While Starr had been plying them all with perfectly grilled steaks and succulent deviled chicken breasts, Stevie had slipped away briefly and come back with goodies of her own. Volumes of erotica she'd plundered from Dragonwood's library—which was even more extensively stocked with titillating literature than the one at Pengilley

Gardens was. And now the doctor and Darryl were studying the books together and laughing and joking as they turned the provocative pages.

She's giving him ideas, the devil! Hettie grinned inwardly at her ingenious friend the doctor. *Working out what they're going to try next!*

And they made a wonderful couple tonight. Stevie so offbeat and sexy in her wacky sportsman's outfit, and Darryl all insouciant and sensual in his muted Italian designer casuals.

He's in good hands, Hettie decided firmly, sipping her strong white wine and realizing she was the very slightest bit tipsy. *We're all in the hands of fate tonight and we'll end up in whatever bed we end up in!*

At one in the morning, Hettie was in her own bed and awake again after an hour's fitful sleep. The night was hot but that wasn't what had wakened her.

Her bed looked like a battlefield. The quilt was on the floor, her old-fashioned white linen sheets were all tangled and crumpled down by her feet and her black satin nightshirt was tangled around her waist. But what had really woken her up was her own hand, jammed between her thighs, fingers furiously working. She couldn't remember any dreams but if there had been any their content was obvious.

The funny thing was, she hadn't felt all that horny when she'd gone to bed. Nobody had, it seemed. They'd all retired their own separate ways with sleepy "goodnights" and nothing more erotic than a peck on the cheek.

She felt turned on now though, her clitoris swollen to the

touch and the whole of her sex engorged and aching. Why hadn't she just orgasmed in her sleep? What was it that had woken her? Withdrawing her sticky fingers, she sat up in bed and listened to the night.

Nothing. Well, nothing unusual or unnatural. There was the hoot of an owl from the woods, the rustle of trees and the fluttering of the lace curtains at the open French window but nothing making noises that shouldn't be making them.

Hettie shivered in spite of the heat, her alerted sixth sense playing games with her imagination. Someone was calling to her. Silently calling… Sending a message to her sex not her ears. And the answer was wet and glistening on her thighs. Feeling strangely wonderful but also uncomfortable, she slid her legs over the side of the bed and stood up.

Barefoot, she padded out of the room through the French window and onto the balcony. All the bedrooms on this side of the house opened onto this veranda and she could see two other sets of curtains fluttering like pantomime ghosts in the brilliant moonlight. Two other sets of French windows were open to the fresh night air and without consciously thinking or choosing, she tiptoed to the one on her right.

When she stepped soundless over the threshold the sight inside brought a grin to her lips.

Great minds and libidos think alike.

In a shaft of moonlight, Stevie was sprawled naked and uncovered on her bed with both her elegant hands clasped tightly between her legs. She was clearly fast asleep, but the smile on her face and the occasional sensuous undulation of her body said that the dream she was having was sensational! A magazine lay on the bed beside her open at nude male centerfold, and Hettie wondered if the hunk depicted there was the source of her friend's nocturnal pleasure—or whether it was someone much closer to home!

Someone only the length of a balcony away.

In Darryl's bedroom the picture illuminated by his bedside lamp was somewhat different. If he was having erotic dreams they were of gentler, less turbulent kind than the doctor's. He looked utterly relaxed and the peace and freshness of his smooth handsome face was strangely affecting. Noiselessly blowing him a kiss, Hettie walked stealthily back out onto the balcony.

But somebody or something had woken her up and as she looked out from the veranda towards the gardens, the shimmering pool and the moonlit terrace, the sight of a familiar and motionless figure was the answer to both her question and her sexual restlessness.

Negotiating the narrow steps at the far end of the balcony, Hettie descended to ground level. Once there she walked as silently as she could along the short path to the terrace, keeping to the grassy edge rather than the gravel. She felt deliciously aware that there was only a short and very sheer silk nightshirt between her heated skin and the mystery of the night.

When her feet felt cool stone beneath them, she paused, undecided. The man leaning on the parapet looked even more aloof than ever and she wondered if he would resent her breaking into his solitude. But when he lifted a cut glass tumbler to his lips and took a sip of its contents, she began to move slowly forward. She guessed that it was scotch in his glass, and this was someone who rarely if ever drank spirits. The only time she'd seen him drink scotch before was the day that Piers had died.

"Beautiful night, isn't it, ma'am?" Starr observed conversationally, although Hettie was convinced she hadn't done a single thing that would have given her away.

"Yes, Starr, it is," she answered, moving towards him

and out into the area where the terrace lamps added extra luminosity. Nervous and excited, she tugged at the hem of her nightshirt. It came barely a quarter of the way down her thighs and she wore no panties beneath it. The mischievous breeze seemed to stiffen and flick at the material, not to mention the moist and tender tissues of her pussy.

Starr was still fully clothed, although his silky black shirt was unfastened and its tails pulled out of his jeans. Hettie noticed that he was barefoot as she was and found the sight of his strong narrow feet almost unbearably erotic. His naked chest shone pale gold in the blended light and she felt a powerful urge to kiss his skin. To lick and bite his small dark nipples. Didn't he realize what a turn-on he was, standing there with his whisky and his silent passion, his pure, hot, unselfish lust unquenched? It was so obvious to her now why he was drinking.

"Couldn't you sleep?" she inquired, cautiously edging closer and almost swearing she could feel his heat.

"I've a few things I need to mull over," he answered, the very noncommittal nature of his answer revealing. He drained the last of his whisky, his long throat undulating, then put the glass down on the parapet.

"What things?"

"Nothing that should worry you, milady." She could feel him retreating, mentally running for a bolt-hole even though he stood perfectly still.

Damn him! He *did* care! He'd already revealed that. There was something there as well as the sex, even though at present the sex seemed to be tamped down as well.

And he looked so gorgeous in the moonlight, so hard and graven. Implacable. Remorseless. A dominator. A man to surrender to and be humble before. This was no servant, despite his claims. That was just another of his masks. His irresistible erotic masks. Without thinking she took that last step forward and lifted her face for a kiss.

He gave the kiss with all the power and ruthlessness that he'd displayed in his bedroom, his whisky-tasting tongue plunging deeply into her mouth as he drew her into his arms and let his hands rove freely over her body, displacing the filmy silk of her nightshirt.

Hettie felt shamelessly wanton as she writhed against him and let her own hand travel over his back and the muscular rounds of his cloth-covered buttocks. He was so ironclad, so immovable sometimes, and it brought out the worst in her now—and the best. She wanted to shock him, offer him something so extreme and intense that it would shake his senses and crack the wall of reserve he'd built around himself.

When his fingers closed around her own soft buttocks, she shimmied against him, wiggling her bottom in his grip to show him how much she enjoyed it. His fingertips got the message and delicately stroked her crease, caressing her through the insubstantial silk. Hettie felt moisture slide heavily down her thigh as her body responded to his indecent probing at her rear. She parted her legs and rubbed her crotch on the unyielding muscle of his thigh, drenching the black fabric of his close-fitting jeans.

Unwinding her arms from around him, she opened the front of her nightshirt and then pressed her breasts against his naked chest. He mumbled something deep in his throat, and though the word was muffled she felt the vibrations through the burning tips of her nipples as she ground them against him.

"Milady. Come on," he urged against her lips, between the devouring kisses. "Let me take you to your room."

Hettie wanted to scream in triumph. He was so hungry, so frantic, so hard as a rock against her belly.

"No," she said tightly, using his own hunger against him. "Here! I want you here! Now! Immediately!" There were other ways of being a "mistress" than simply being driven around or waited on or cooked for.

As ever, he obeyed, and she could see the same daring fire in his eyes that she knew must be lighting up her own. It wasn't obedience she saw there. Far from it. *He* wanted the danger and outrage of it just as much as she did. There was a delicious ruthlessness in his fingers as he slid them into her sex and started rubbing her clitoris hard and fast.

She moaned and clung to him, her bottom pressed against the parapet as he rocked against her using the weight of his own body to add momentum to his ravaging fingers. Hettie could feel her juices pouring out onto his hand. She was inundating him and almost embarrassed that her readiness was so blatant.

"Starr, please!" she hissed, half plea, half command. She ached to be filled and stretched, to be splayed wide open. She wanted to be taken rudely. Primitively. She wanted to stop being "milady" and just be breasts and sex and ass for him to use and possess exactly as he wished.

His answer was to carry on fingering her. Circling her clitoris, slicking between her slippery labia, then pressing one then two then three digits inside her. She moaned, wanting more, much more.

With an incoherent cry of his own, a noise not like Starr at all, he grabbed her by the hips, placed her poised on the edge of the parapet and then swiftly and deftly unzipped himself. He took a half second to free himself from his underwear, and then his cock was out and pointing at her, huge and red and fierce, its tip dripping, the slit open and distended. With great care, he eased her further forward and put her legs right over his shoulders, positioning himself perfectly, right against her sex. There was another cry—his or hers, she didn't know and couldn't tell—and then in a long smooth power lunge he was in her right to the hilt.

Hettie felt her inner walls tighten and grip him hungrily at the very moment her body started tipping backwards. There was an instant of crazy falling vertigo then Starr's strong arm was at the nape of her neck controlling the rate of her tilt.

With infinite gentleness he eased her down onto the stone, the back of her head just resting on the broad parapet, her hair hanging loose and free in the air. She felt him place his hand flat on the slab beneath her scalp, making a pillow for her head with his fingers while his other hand returned to her clitoris. For her own part, she scrabbled wildly at anything. The parapet. Starr's arms. His back. Anything to grant her purchase against his thrusts.

And thrust he did, sliding into her doubled up body, his cock going deep into her loins. It was fabulous and she shouted as an immediate orgasm claimed her, her clitoris and womb beating in time as the controlled force of his onslaught ground her bottom against the stone of the parapet. She would have grazes tomorrow but tomorrow was centuries and light-years away.

For minutes on end she orgasmed almost continuously, crying and groaning like an animal gripped by pure pleasure. She was conscious of him iron-hard right inside her, his erection unfaltering, un-waning, almost inhuman.

In the midst of it, she experienced a second of lucidity. *He can go on forever like this! He still hasn't come, lost it or ceded even the tiniest scrap of his self-control, the bastard.*

Even while she continued to orgasm around him, she started to wriggle more purposefully in his grip, consumed by the idea of something that would really blow his mind—if he'd do it. If he'd let her give him that gift.

"Starr!" she gasped, snatching at a lull between climaxes to reach him. "Starr, let me up! I want something different. I want to turn over!"

In a long wet slide, he pulled out of her then took her ankles from behind his ears and gently levered them to the ground. Vaguely aware that her bottom was tender and that her nightshirt was shredded to pieces, Hettie flipped over quickly and lay facedown on the parapet. Her pussy was swimming with love juices and the whole of her sex and the groove of her bottom were awash with it. She was perfectly lubricated. There would never be a better moment or a set of conditions more opportune.

Reaching behind herself, she pulled apart the cheeks of her backside and bared the little opening there that was slithery, pouting and ready.

"I want you here, Starr!" she purred, injecting every ounce of "Lady Henrietta" into her voice. He'd balk at this, she knew. They'd never done it. But equally it was just the intense, dark, unthinkable act she needed to smash through his barriers and bend his rigid internal discipline.

"Milady... Are you sure?" His voice was shaky and Hettie felt a rush of intoxicating female power. She waved her behind in his face, taunting and inviting.

"Just do it, Starr!" she decreed, almost orgasming on the pure need to be possessed so completely. The idea that she could have him inside her bottom, take his seed there and blow his cool analytical mind.

He made a small sound of acquiescence—a sort of respectful growl—then she felt him touching her between her legs again, scooping up her wetness and bringing it to her bottom. He did this once, twice, three times and only then did he seem satisfied she was slick enough.

Carefully, almost as if she were made of porcelain, he positioned himself, and Hettie quivered wildly when she felt the tip of him stroke against her. He was still silently hesitating, still checking she was sure and comfortable, but in an imperious motion she bucked her body backwards and compelled him to continue. Reaching back awkwardly, she pried herself further open and the long, slow indecent pressure began.

It was a riot of strange stimulation and not what she'd expected at all. There seemed to be an iron club as wide a Starr's fist trying to enter her and a simmering, burning sensation spread out from the dilating ring of her anus and engulfed the whole of her bottom and her sex. Unspeakable messages shrieked along her nerves from the inside of her ass—sly, disgusting urges that flared to a peak where she was convinced that any second the unthinkable would happen. But then, mercifully, they ebbed away just as quickly.

After what seemed an age of shuffling, pushing and adjusting, Hettie found herself draped over the parapet like a half-broken doll, her sex on fire but empty and her ass plumbed to the very depths by Starr's hugely throbbing cock. She could feel him pulsating inside her, his size unforgiving and his heat incredible. It was like having a red-hot sword in her bowels.

It was out of this world.

With a bubbling moan she came enormously and felt moisture ooze from her forsaken sex and pool on the stone beneath her. Keeping one hand on the parapet to steady herself, she reached under their combined weight with the other and jerked ruthlessly at her pulsing clitoris. She could hear herself howling but had no idea how her throat was making the sounds. She squirmed frantically as Starr began to move inside her, the dark threats stirring faintly again, but this time she didn't give a damn what happened as long as the voluptuous pleasure in her bottom continued to another incendiary, climactic conclusion.

"Go on, Starr, do it!" she hissed as he plunged into her. "It's wonderful! Do it! Do it! Do it!"

"Oh God! Oh God!" he gasped in her ear, the words forced out between gritted teeth. Words that became jumbled. Barely coherent.

Oh, you beautiful man!

On the thought, her pussy spasmed again and she came in glory as she heard her name at last on his lips. Distinct as a prayer.

"Hettie!"

Her sex was a melting ball of ecstasy, her clitoris as bright as the heart of a galaxy, but suddenly she could think and reason and act. In a supreme effort of will, a fight against her own orgasming body, she gripped his cock with her bottom, tightening her insulted sphincter to embrace, caress and love the inflexible rod inside her. Holding him snugly she rolled her hips and scissored her thighs against his, then contracted her anus again and again in a slow rhythmic pump on his enclosed organ.

With a great shout of, "Oh Hettie, I adore you!" the man inside her climaxed too, flooding her rectum with a warm delicious outpouring of semen that felt like a holy healing potion to the battered interior of her ass.

Hettie sobbed as he overwhelmed her, her own sex convulsing again in an orgasm that was strangely mild and gentle. Just one soft pulse of her clitoris under her finger, one long, internal flutter and she was completely and utterly sated. Even as she breathed out Starr's name in gratitude, she felt her body cooling, relaxing and calming beneath him.

As he softened inside her, then slid out to rest in her ass

cleft, Hettie felt a great rush of tenderness for the mighty thing that'd been inside her so rudely and yet was now so shrunken and defenseless. She wanted to tell him this, describe the emotion, but words didn't seem adequate. And her ability to speak was robbed completely when Starr turned his face against her neck and she felt moisture anoint her skin.

Tears? Tears for me?

She wept herself. Wept for joy and for pleasure. Wept for the revelation that her strong, imperturbable lover felt enough for her to cry.

"Wake up, Darryl! Wake up! It's important!"

The soft urgent voice dragged Darryl from the depths of sleep. Blinking furiously, he looked up into the face of the woman who was shaking him and tried to work out just what was going on.

As his consciousness cleared, he couldn't help but smile.

It was Stevie, the beautiful, amazing, provocative goddess of sex who'd given her body so generously to him that very afternoon. She seemed to be doing her utmost to rouse him, and in more ways than one. She was slightly sleep-disheveled and deliciously young-looking tonight, with rumpled hair and a fresh, unmade-up face. Her stylish man's dressing gown was very haphazardly belted, and with a happy sigh, he reached for her, instantly ready for more of the wonders they'd shared earlier.

"In a little while, greedy thing!" she whispered, mock-stern. "There's something you've got to see first. Something you might learn something from. Come on! Out of bed. Or we'll miss all the best bits."

Rubbing his eyes, Darryl obeyed her, trying not to groan aloud at the burning ache in his fiercely erect cock. It hadn't taken much to bring him to full hardness, but Stevie's nearness, and the thought of whatever those "best bits" might be seemed to be making him even more rigid.

It must be Hettie and Starr.

Acutely aware that his hard-on was making a huge tent in his pajama bottoms, he shoved his feet into his slippers and then allowed Stevie to take him by the hand and lead him onto the balcony. The full moon was very bright, and he saw his companion's rosy mouth quirk into a broad smile at the sight of his condition.

"Sorry," he muttered, not feeling sorry at all, but Stevie "shushed" him with a finger to her lips and gave him a wicked wink that played havoc with agony in his groin.

Like a pair of cat burglars, they crept along the balcony, keeping to the shadows, until they reached a spot where they had a good view of the terrace while remaining hidden themselves.

Darryl felt his mouth drop open. Below them a vision of erotic drama was unfolding.

They're fucking! Dio mio, *they're fucking!*

It was what he'd expected to see, but the reality far exceeded even his wildest, most detailed fantasies.

Hettie lay on the stone parapet, almost doubled up beneath Starr, who was thrusting into her with a manic desperation. The tall blond was a strong man, and he seemed to be using every last ounce of that strength to hurl himself into the body of the woman he loved. The woman who was clutching at him, twisting about beneath him, shouting and crying out while her lover fucked her with almost superhuman power.

As the couple down below writhed and bucked

against each other, Darryl's hand flew to his groin and his monumental erection.

But before he could free himself from his pajamas, a smaller, more nimble hand had negotiated the fly and eased his cock out into the open.

Darryl bit down on his lip. He sincerely doubted that Hettie and Starr would hear any sound he uttered, but he daren't take the chance of shouting out aloud. Stevie's elegant fingers curled around him and began a slow, swirling, tormenting dance that almost made him forget what he was watching.

Squeeze. Slide. Squeeze.

It was all done so teasingly, so calculatedly. The glide of Stevie's fingertips seemed to be synchronized with Starr's thrusts as he powered into Hettie down on the parapet.

Darryl felt as if he was going to pass out. That, or shoot his cum into the empty air in front of him. He tasted blood in his mouth as he struggled for control. Then nearly lost it completely when he felt Stevie's other hand pushing his pajama trousers down at the back. A second later, there was bare skin against his bare skin, and the soft, silky tickle of her bush against his bottom and the back of his thighs as she rocked herself against him.

Afraid that he'd fall, Darryl grasped the railing in front of him. He no longer cared if the couple on the terrace knew that they were being watched. He didn't think it was likely, although he could barely think at all.

He couldn't hear properly, for the pounding of blood in his ears, but as Stevie began to do something intricate and devilish to the head of his cock, he realized that Hettie was speaking to Starr, her voice breathy yet somehow also imperious. The words were indecipherable, but her intention was clear. A second later, Starr withdrew, and the beautiful woman wriggled around beneath him, and turned over on the stone surface.

What now? Oh, what now?

Feeling as if he were going mad and had stumbled into the most intense sex dream he could possibly have imagined, Darryl watched, his arms and his thighs shaking with tension, as the couple below rearranged themselves into new symmetry that was both beautiful and perverse.

Clad only in the rags of a black silk nightshirt, Hettie was offering a rare gift to the blond man who loved her. Opening herself in a way that Darryl hardly dare think about. If he did imagine what that dark, forbidden penetration might feel like, he knew—he knew for certain—that he'd come immediately.

Darryl shut his eyes and surrendered himself to sensation rather than the extreme vision of sensuality down below him.

"What's wrong, sweetheart?" Stevie's voice was scarcely more than a breath against his naked shoulder.

"I-I can't watch," Darryl gasped, feeling her fingers grow still on his cock. Involuntarily, his hips jerked as if his body were urging her of its own accord to continue fondling him. "It's just too much. If I look at them any longer, I'll just come!"

"Is that such a bad thing?"

"But I want..." His voice simply failed him. He didn't know what he wanted other than to climax. Somewhere at the back of his brain, a small voice was telling him that he shouldn't be selfish, and that he should think of Stevie's pleasure too. But that chivalrous whisper was being drowned out by the baying of his primal sex drive, the screaming and shouting for immediate orgasm.

"Watch them!"

Darryl could not honestly say whether he'd actually

heard the words, or whether Stevie had suddenly acquired telepathic powers. All he knew that in the instant he opened his eyes, the sweet warmth of her bare body was withdrawn from his back and buttocks and her hand released his penis. He felt a moment of excruciating loss, then his heart leapt as he realized what Stevie was up to.

Darryl was in no doubt that below, on the parapet, Starr was buggering Hettie, but up here, on the balcony, there was an equal wonder.

Stevie had sunk nimbly to her knees, and scooted around to fit her lithe body in between him and the balcony railing. His teeth dug fiercely into his lip again as heavenly heat and moisture enveloped his burning cock, and a flexible muscular tongue began to work pure magic on him.

His thighs went rigid and the tendons in his arms seemed to pop as he fought to not fill Stevie's mouth with his semen almost instantaneously. The sensation of being sucked and licked and tantalized was out of this world, and even while his body clamored for release, he was filled with an enormous rush of gratitude. He suddenly wanted to kiss the beautiful woman who was pleasuring him so unselfishly, yet at the same time, he knew he was beyond anything but coming in her exquisite mouth at any second.

Yes, he wanted to come, just as Starr and Hettie were coming. The couple below were bucking and jerking against each other, and crying out now, the sounds unearthly, almost animal, yet obviously expressions of great love. Darryl heard Starr shout, "Oh Hettie, I adore you!" then suddenly it seemed to be over as the tall, black-clad man collapsed over the back of his beloved.

It was too much, too beautiful to behold, and like Starr, Darryl finally lost control. His spine seemed to melt and he climaxed helplessly into the sweet, liquid warmth of Stevie's mouth. His hips pumped furiously, but with a supreme effort he suppressed his own cry of triumph. Inside though, he howled out a litany of praise for the lovely, generous woman who was pleasuring him. He knew he didn't love Stevie as Starr loved Hettie, but he *did* care, and she would always be precious to him.

And pretty soon, when he recovered, he would use everything she'd taught him to give her pleasure in return.

Chapter Eight

Hettie woke late the next morning. The sun was already riding high when she turned over in her tangled sheets, shivering deliciously as her body reminded her of what'd happened in the middle of the night.

She'd got off amazingly lightly all things considered. Her nightshirt was in tatters but there were only a couple of small grazes on her bottom and some light scratches on her thighs and breasts. It was a miracle considering the raw power that Starr had expended in making love to her. How passionately he'd taken her—in both her sensual orifices.

The thought of him made her go hot and cold. Hot at the thought of the pleasure, the wildness, the almost transcendental quality of his lovemaking. Cold at the fact that he might well draw away from what they'd shared and become his old self again. That when he next appeared, he might be as remote and emotionally insulated as he always was.

Where are you now, you bastard?

Rolling over in her bed, she felt a great lift in her spirits when she realized where he had been not long ago.

There was cup of tea on her bedside table and when she

reached gratefully for it, the brew was fresh and hot and steaming. Starr had stood at the side of this bed perhaps a minute before she'd woken.

What'd passed through his mind as he'd looked down on her? She knew now that he *did* have feelings for her. He had to feel something. He was far too honest to fake and last night he'd groaned and wept and fucked with a force and fury that'd taken her breath away.

For her own part, she was in turmoil. Even if Starr was able to compartmentalize what he felt, last night's glories had touched Hettie more profoundly than she dare admit.

She had felt as if she'd opened not only her body but also her soul to him. She felt vulnerable and submissive in a way she'd never felt before. It was what they'd done, she supposed, sipping her perfect tea. The intensity and darkness of it. In an act more intimate than straightforward fucking, you had to trust more, allow more and reveal more. She'd put her faith in him and he'd cherished her in a way that was both fiery and delicate. Great swirls of emotion rushed through her, and in her secret heart, she hugged her love and cherished it.

Soon, Starr! Soon I'll tell you!

The idea of finally revealing more than her physical self gave her an exhilarating rush of energy.

When she was showered and dressed in a black thong bikini and filmy cheesecloth overshirt, she considered what to do with the garment that'd been ruined last night.

The nightshirt was in shreds both back and front, yet Hettie couldn't bear to throw it away even though it was far beyond any kind of repair. She held it to her face and smelt an intoxicating cocktail of odors. Her own perfume and the mingled sexual sweat of two bodies that had performed with passionate vigor. She could smell her own arousal and the sharp distinctive note of semen.

She could even see his essence. White streaks plain and telling on the thin black satin. Folding the shirt almost reverently, she slid it into her drawer, knowing she would never discard it and probably never wash it. Starr had revealed a lot of himself last night and she would always treasure this ragged black reminder.

But where was the man who'd shredded the shirt?

Shall I go to him? Seek him out? Test the bond we forged last night in the harsh light of day?

Closing her eyes for a moment, she sent out a silent mental query. She didn't believe in ESP and telepathy and other mumbo jumbo, but even so she felt a connection between them shiver like an invisible silver cord. He was close by, with her yet not with her. For the moment it seemed unnecessary to compel his physical presence. That would come later. For the moment she felt an urge to seek out her friends—one old, one new—and see how they were faring.

Both Stevie and Darryl had beaten her to the terrace, but obviously not by much because they were both still lingering over coffee and the remnants of their breakfast. Plates bearing toast crusts and melon peel still lay on the floor beside their loungers.

Stevie sat up and smiled, her eyes hidden behind her dark sunglasses. "You're late, sweetheart," she observed with a faint but enigmatic emphasis. "Are you okay?"

"Yes, I'm fine!" replied Hettie, realizing that she was. Much more than fine. Her body was a bit battered, but it still bore the resonance of some truly remarkable lovemaking. With a truly remarkable man.

"Good morning, Hettie."

Darryl was on his feet before her, gorgeous as ever in his brief black swimming trunks and with an expression that could only be described as awe in his shining brown eyes. Before she could frame even the simplest answer, he'd reached out, taken her hand and drawn it to his lips in a salute that was as fervent as it was unexpected.

What's going on?

Unnerved, Hettie allowed Darryl to get her a cup of coffee from the fresh pot that was perking there.

"Do you want something to eat, love?" inquired Stevie, slipping off her sunglasses and giving a Hettie a long, narrow-eyed look that managed to be both kind and assessing the same time.

"No. No, thanks. I'm not really hungry. I didn't sleep well... I might have something later..." She was almost stammering as a sudden and totally outrageous thought occurred then coalesced into an absolute certainty.

They know! Somehow they know what happened here last night.

Without thinking she glanced towards the parapet, the stone altar where she'd spread her body in a willing sacrifice to Starr. When she looked back, Stevie was still regarding her steadily. And Darryl still looked as if he were prepared to fall down at her feet and worship her!

They saw it! They must have! They must have heard all the yelling and come out here to investigate.

Hettie felt a blush start rising up her chest and throat. A roaring panic surged in her heart, then died again just as fast. For all its raunchiness and indecency, what had passed between her and Starr had been beautiful. An act of immense sensuality, and yet an act of love. A series of couplings to be proud of, to glory in and to thrill others with by letting them watch.

She looked first at Stevie then at Darryl and though it was just too much to tell them outright in words, she used her eyes to let them know that she didn't mind.

Stevie smiled, and Darryl *still* looked awestruck. Gazing back at them, Hettie felt a new surge run through her but not of panic this time. It was an odd sensation, an amalgam of affection and a strange erotic kinship. This beautiful woman and the equally beautiful man beside her were her comrades in sex somehow, and she felt a sudden sharp surge of fondness for them. Starr was still with her, a silent but permanent resident in her heart and her imagination, but her thoughts and memories of him didn't make either Darryl or Stevie one bit less appealing.

"So what have you two been doing?" she inquired carefully, taking a sip of her coffee then sinking down onto a lounger in the shady part of the terrace.

"Drinking Buck's Fizz. Waiting for you. Discussing life…and sex," Stevie replied with a frank grin, sliding off her voluminous overshirt as she spoke and revealing that all she had on underneath was a pair of tiny high-cut denim shorts. They were bleached almost white and so frayed at the legs that when Stevie flipped elegantly over onto her stomach, her pale, sleek buttocks were almost completely exposed.

"Is that a fact?" Hettie said softly. She nearly asked what Darryl thought of Stevie's choice of conversation, but it was quite obvious. His skimpy trunks hid as little as Stevie's ragamuffin shorts did, and Hettie could see the clear evidence of an erection rising beneath them.

He grinned at her, and she felt sex swirl lazily through her loins as the hot as the morning sun beat down on the canopy above them. She felt horny, but completely passive.

Maybe it's my turn to be the watcher now?

The thought amused her. After all, she'd provided the floorshow last night, out here on this very patio with Starr. Let the good doctor and her pupil provide the entertainment this time. And then later, someone else would reap the benefits—when she found him...

"Let's have some of that Buck's Fizz." She glanced across at the smiling, half-naked Stevie. "If the good doctor hasn't drunk it all."

"Don't worry I can easily mix some more," said Stevie, uncoiling herself from her resting place and making for the table.

Stevie's hand with the champagne was more than generous.

"There's more fizz than buck in this," gasped Hettie, recklessly swallowing down another mouthful of the delicious concoction. With her stomach unlined, the champagne had an immediate and potent effect, and she could almost feel Stevie studying her intently across the lip of her own freshly filled glass.

Hettie began to feel drowsy again, from the effect of her fine wine not so hidden within the orange juice and the tumultuous night with its shortfall of sleep. She took another small sip of the Buck's Fizz and then settled down upon her lounger again. "It's so hot already," she murmured. "I don't know about you two but I could do with a snooze."

Stevie laughed but said nothing. Her impish wink was more eloquent than words.

Lying facedown, Hettie cradled her head on her folded arms, and let her eyelids drift downward and the perfumed warmth of the golden day embrace her. Beginning to float, she imagined Starr touching her lightly—not in ferocious passion as last night, but gently, tenderly, reverently and with the love she knew he bore her. The love that was a mirror of her own. He might not have said anything just yet. And he might not say anything for a while. But Hettie knew that eventually he'd declare himself.

In her pleasant haze, she focused in on snippets of conversation drifting from across the patio. Stevie and Darryl were whispering, laughing, murmuring naughty secrets and totally intent on each other. They were having a marvelous time—a blast—flirting outrageously and making little threats and promises.

You've come a long way in such a few days, Signor di Angeli.

Hettie smiled indulgently at Darryl as a potent silence settled over the patio.

After a little while, she opened her eyes a smidgen and sneaked a look at the mischievous pair.

And almost gasped out loud…

Darryl and Stevie were entwined on one of the mattresses spread out on the warm stone. They were kissing passionately now, their mouths dueling and their hands all over each other's bodies.

As she regarded them from beneath her lashes, she saw Stevie wriggle sinuously against Darryl while she pulled off her shorts and then tossed them away. A second later, she'd drawn his hand between her thighs and adjusted her hips to position his fingers in exactly the right position to give her pleasure.

"That's right, sweetheart," she crooned, as Darryl began to kiss her throat while he fingered her, "Rub me just there… Ooh, that's wonderful! That's so good!"

It was an intoxicating sight. The slender man, all tanned and lean with his cock barely contained in an abbreviated swimsuit, and the shapely doctor completely naked, with breasts, thighs, belly and pussy all on show. Stevie's hips jerked rhythmically and she was grunting now. The sounds were raw and primal as they drifted towards Hettie, who lay entranced by the sight of the embracing couple. She felt a tiny pang of envy.

How delicious it would be to be caressed like that, and for a moment she imagined that it was herself and Starr she was viewing, and her own impassioned voice crying out. Starr's golden body was inclined over her and her paler thighs were parted to admit his questing hand.

And then, gorgeous as it was, the vision faded. And reality, just as erotic, held her gaze.

As the couple writhed, Stevie whispered something into Darryl's ear that made his dark eyebrows shoot up. "Really?" Hettie heard him say, then saw Stevie nod and smile at him, her mouth curved and sultry. A second later they were rearranging their bodies.

First, the good doctor had knelt over the excited Darryl, and performed the most intense, thorough and delicately detailed act of fellatio that Hettie could ever have imagined.

It was like watching a supreme artist at work and Hettie found herself noting certain tricks, then imagining how she herself could perform them for Starr. Wondering if she could extract the same groans and shouts of agonized fulfillment from him that Stevie was inducing in Darryl. And afterward, when Darryl returned the compliment for the doctor, Hettie could only remember Starr's mouth on her sex and his tongue lashing her beleaguered clitoris with far more craft and assurance than Darryl would probably be capable of for a long, long time…

Oh Starr, where are you? The sudden need to be near him rose up again. Like a pain that only he could soothe.

Discreetly, she rose and excused herself even though her two companions were now completely absorbed in one another. Their entwined bodies were a beautiful sight, one that any other occasion she would have lingered over to savor, but she longed for beauty of an entirely different kind.

Cool, perfect, and as hard and brilliantly faceted as a jewel…

Back in her room, she bathed quickly, not wanting to delay in her passionate wish to see Starr again. But just as she'd finished applying moisturizer to her skin in readiness for dressing, there was a soft knock at the door and she knew without the tiniest scrap of doubt that her sudden yearning had been granted.

Starr!

Tall, straight and golden, he walked in at her "Come in!" then closed the door behind him and moved slowly towards the bed. He was clad in black as usual—a tight cotton T-shirt and thigh-hugging jeans—and his blue eyes were as steady as ever.

And yet somewhere far back in his gaze, there was a shadow that told her he was troubled. At one time, she wouldn't have been able to see it, but now she seemed attuned to the very subtlest nuance of his expressions. Either she knew him much better now or perhaps he was finally letting his barriers down at last? Maybe his tears of last night had been a catalyst somehow?

"Are you all right, ma'am? Is there anything I can get you?" he asked quietly. "I saw the doctor downstairs and she said you'd returned to your room. I felt concerned in case… In case…"

Amazingly the calm, collected Starr was faltering. Hettie could barely believe it, but somehow his vulnerability made her heart thunder like a cannonade. He *was* letting down his guard! At last! She'd always trusted him, but maybe now he was finally going to trust her.

"I'm fine, Starr. Thank you. I think it's just that all the good air and sunshine tends to make me sleepy."

It was a white lie. If anything was making her tired, it was the emotional tension that had been building between them. The constant longing to know, to understand… But she sensed that the moment at hand was too delicate for so explicit an explanation. "Please, why don't you sit down a moment?" She patted the white counterpane at her side, almost holding her breath for fear he'd refuse her.

With pure male grace, he complied, sitting down with his lithe body twisted slightly to face her.

Her heart still thudding so hard she could almost imagine he could see it, Hettie met his cool blue eyes and tried to fathom the mystery in their depths. He looked away then— so unlike him—and smoothed a long golden finger along the seam of his jeans. She could sense that he was right on the point of speaking.

"What is it, Starr?" prompted Hettie softly.

He looked up again. Right into her eyes. "About last night, ma'am. I hope I didn't hurt you. I wanted to be gentle… But I couldn't. I wanted you too much."

"You didn't hurt me," she lied quickly, moved by his unflinching honesty. "It was what I wanted. It was marvelous." Without stopping to think or consider, she edged forward and reached up to touch his strong, smooth jawline. Beneath her fingers she felt the faintest hint of stubble and his blue eyes went dark as night as she began to caress him tentatively.

"My lady… My lady…" His voice broke as he surged forward like a panther and in one subtle move had his arms around her body and his mouth hungrily on hers.

For a split second Hettie was too stunned to respond, but as she felt him trying to pull back, her body was galvanized into action.

No, you weren't wrong, Hettie. He loves you as much as you love him!

She willed the thought from her mind into his, backing it up with the force of her mouth as she pushed her tongue hungrily between his lips and kissed him with all the power he'd ever used on her. She felt the vibration of a purr of pleasure in his throat and scrabbled quickly between their bodies to undo her robe and present her naked breasts to his hands.

As he rolled over her, the balance of the kiss tipped again and his tongue fought hers back into her mouth as his fingers formed two natural, cradling curves around her breasts. Lips and tongues dueled moistly as he fondled and kneaded her and Hettie whimpered faintly at the sudden almost grinding heaviness that massed in her loins.

Wriggling furiously, she managed to work the lower half of her robe open and then rocked her pussy against the rigid column of his penis where it pressed through the black denim of his jeans. His thumbs rotated wickedly on her nipples and Hettie surged up against him, her sex fluttering wildly as the simple caress set a spark to her unbearable need and she climaxed involuntarily against his still-clothed crotch.

"Starr! Oh, Starr!" she sobbed, her body still throbbing as he lifted away from her slightly and she felt him working on his belt and his jeans button.

He was fumbling, tugging with a strange, endearing clumsiness at his clothes. "My lady," he gasped. "Oh my lady, I—"

Suddenly there was a heavy pummeling at the door and they both froze in shock. Starr rolled off her instantly, refastening his belt in sharp jerky moves as his blue eyes blazed with what could only be furious anger.

As she righted her robe and tied its sash tightly, Hettie felt both frustrated at the interruption and at the same time strangely thrilled by the fury in Starr's flashing eyes. For a man so controlled and so self-contained, his anger was as revealing to her as his lovemaking would've been.

"Come in!" she called out to whoever it was who was still thumping vigorously on the door.

Darryl almost fell into the room, looking rather worried. "I'm really sorry to disturb you, Hettie, but Cousin Renata's here, and I thought you'd want to see her straightaway. She's very upset and she's not making a lot of sense."

Well, that makes a change, Ren! Hettie instantly chastised herself for the unkind thought and hurried down the stairs, with both the anxiously chattering Darryl and the now silent Starr in her wake.

Darryl was right, but it was the whole situation that didn't make sense. Renata was supposed to be in Milan, besotted and embroiled idyllically with Fausto. *Wasn't that was the very reason you sent Darryl to me in the first place? So you could have time alone with your hot new lover?*

So what the hell was Renata doing here now, hard on the heels of the adoptive cousin she'd just gone to so much trouble to get rid of?

Hettie had tried to phone her friend just before leaving London, hoping to update her on Darryl's progress and check that Ren was still getting on okay with Fausto. But even after several attempts, all Hettie had been able to get was the answering machine. So she'd left a brief message telling Ren that Darryl was fine and that they were all going down to Dragonwood for a country break.

It was obvious now though that something drastic had happened at Palazzo Di Angeli. Something so traumatic that it had caused Renata to flee Italy and come racing straight here to Dragonwood without ever pausing to let anybody know she was even on her way!

The commotion—and the sight of a huge pile of baggage—met them at the foot of the stairs. The sound of loud hysterical weeping, underpinned by a soft soothing murmuring, was emanating from the open doors of the library and a rather bemused-looking taxi driver stood in the middle of the hall. Hettie flashed him a brief smile, and then flung a look of gratitude towards Starr when the tall blond nodded to indicate that she should tend to her friend while he dealt with the cab fare.

"Ren, what on earth's the matter?" Hettie said as she sprinted across the library towards the wailing and blubbering young woman who was sitting on one of the leather-covered sofas.

Renata di Angeli was hunched and miserable, her pretty face streaked with mascara and her eyes red and puffy. Stevie was beside her, talking calmly and offering tissues and a glass of brandy. She didn't seem to be making much headway though, because the Italian girl was quite beside herself.

Hettie knelt on the carpet in front of her friend and took hold of her shaking hands. "Calm down, love, please! Take it easy. Drink a sip of brandy." Stevie held out the glass. "Tell us what's the matter."

The presence of more people in the room would have fazed Hettie even more, but strangely it seemed to have a calming effect on Renata. Still sniffing and hiccupping, she finally took the proffered brandy glass and swallowed a small mouthful. Then after another spate of coughing and spluttering and a well-placed slap on the back from Stevie, she finally managed to get a hold of herself. As Darryl slid onto the seat beside her and tenderly took hold of her hand, she even managed a wan smile.

"It's Fausto. He's left me. He was furious…" She turned suddenly towards Darryl and Hettie was astounded by the way his gentle smile seemed to soothe the distraught woman.

"He was so angry, *caro*," she said to him softly. "The same day you left, some lawyers came. They told us about all the money that Uncle left you. Then Fausto went crazy because I'd found somewhere else for you to live." She bit her lip, her face a picture of guilt.

"He said I was a stupid bitch and that if you'd stayed, he could've persuaded you to invest in his business." She turned miserably towards Hettie. "He was only after money. He was furious because mine's all tied up in trusts. When he found out he couldn't get it, he said I was useless. Boring…" Her lip started quivering again and suddenly she was crying as hard as before. "He said I was frigid. Like a log of wood. The worst lay he'd ever had!"

Hettie's heart ached for her friend, but just as she was reaching up to comfort her, Darryl swept the weeping woman into his arms and began to stroke and cuddle and soothe her. He held her with all the tender, kindly assurance of someone who had a lifetime's knowledge of counseling and comforting unhappy women.

Hettie looked up, not quite sure what to do, her own eyes panning from Stevie to the newly arrived Starr in search of a course of action.

The doctor nodded in the direction of the entwined di Angelis, confirming Hettie's suspicion that Darryl was probably the best man for the job at the moment. Starr looked on calmly, his own inner turmoil apparently forgotten, then shrugged a tacit agreement with Stevie's split-second analysis.

Hettie rose quietly to her feet and gestured in his direction. "Come on, Starr. Let's sort out a room for Ren. I assume all those bags in the hall are hers. God knows how she got all that into a taxi!"

As she and Starr moved soft-footedly from the room, Stevie got up and followed them. "If you two are getting a room ready, the least I can do is prepare some food," she said, turning in the direction of the kitchen.

Starr frowned slightly, and Hettie felt momentary amusement—despite the crisis—when Stevie tossed him a defiant look in response.

"Okay, so I'm not the world's greatest cook, but if there's a chainsaw handy, I can probably manage some sandwiches!" She didn't actually thumb her nose as she strode off across the hall, but the implication was certainly there.

Hettie smiled as she made her way back up the stairs with Starr once more at her heels.

She chose a small but prettily decorated room for Renata, and it wasn't long before they were engaged in the strangely silent task of making the bed together. A hundred questions rose to Hettie's lips but each time, she held her tongue and got on with the job at hand because Starr seemed as remote and masked as he'd ever been. It was as if the revealing moments of earlier had never taken place, although inside her own heart, Hettie couldn't erase them.

As Starr worked deftly beside her she could do nothing but wish he would grab hold of her and lay her down on the bed, crushing the sheets they'd just smoothed as he made sudden, urgent love to her. The robe she wore seemed so insubstantial, so precarious. It would be the simplest thing in the world to shrug it off and offer her naked body to him, here on this bed. To open her legs and guide him inside her so his cock could assuage the hunger that grew and grew in her flesh with every second that passed.

But it wasn't to be. The room prepared, Starr silently led the way out onto the landing, his strong face as shuttered and expressionless as ever.

Hettie felt an inner chaos of conflicting emotions. If Renata hadn't arrived, there was no knowing what would've happened. Starr had been just on the point of possessing her, but Hettie's every feminine instinct told her that the moment of greatest revelation had been imminent too. The word that had stilled on his lips had been unmistakable.

And now Ren was here and the atmosphere was shattered, the momentous turning point temporarily lost. The selfish part of Hettie felt furious, while the soft, tenderhearted side of her was desperately sorry for the Italian girl. Another sexual disaster! Poor Ren's confidence must be at rock bottom.

And yet there was still a green shoot of hope. It was obvious that Renata had responded to Darryl's gentleness. Which was ironic when Ren had recently been so anxious to get rid of him. But it did look amazingly as if the two di Angelis had a genuine bond and might be meant to look after each other after all.

And you, mister, are supposed to look after me!

She hurled the words silently at the fast-retreating Starr as he made his way down the stairs and she returned to her own room to put on something less revealing and far less evocative than the short robe that she'd so recently opened for his pleasure.

"And love me," she added softly, clinging to hope…

Chapter Nine

It was another golden morning at Dragonwood.
Hettie woke early, but realized that she obviously wasn't the first to think about rising. Even as she rubbed her eyes, someone was tapping on the door.

Last night had been subdued for one and all. No sensual encounters, no sneaking into rooms, no passion on the parapet. No sex of any kind, it seemed.

Exhausted by her journey, Renata had retired early, and to Hettie's acute disappointment Starr had kept to himself too, reassuming his role as the discreet, invisible servant.

She and Stevie and Darryl had watched television, although none of them had really seemed to pay a lot of attention to what should have been a side-splittingly funny film. Finally they'd all gone to bed early—and by unspoken agreement—alone. As she sat up and reached for a robe to cover her thin slip of a nightdress, Hettie wondered if the others had experienced dreams as troubled as she had.

"Come in!" she called out when the visitor rapped again, her heart skittering wildly even though it didn't sound like Starr's firm assured knock.

Stevie entered, bearing a cup of tea. To Hettie's surprise,

her friend was fully clothed and immaculate in a smart pinstriped suit. The doctor was dressed for travel, that much was obvious.

"Yes, love, I'm on my way," she said in answer to Hettie's unspoken question. "My work here is done now, Hettie. I'm surplus to requirements, so I'm driving back to London and my patients."

Agitated, Hettie took a sip of tea, then put down the cup as she tried to frame something adequate to say. To find a voice for the tangle of thoughts, and the compelling feeling that somehow Stevie was right.

"But we need you more than ever, Stevie. You're a psychologist and a trained counselor, after all, and Ren's in such a state. You're exactly the person we *do* need!"

Stevie shook her head and sat down on the bed. In spite of everything, Hettie felt the same old familiar *frisson* at the other woman's nearness, the same surge of excitement that someone could be so different, so female and yet so strangely desirable. When Stevie reached for her hand, she gave it gladly.

"Thank you, sweetheart," said Stevie softly, giving Hettie's fingers a squeeze, then releasing them. "But I had a chance to talk to Renata yesterday afternoon, and I think what she actually needs most right now is a bit of tender loving care." The older woman shrugged, and glanced quickly and wistfully at the hand she'd just released. "From Darryl."

It was the conclusion that Hettie had come to as well, despite the fact of Darryl's relative inexperience. "That's quite an achievement, Stevie. You've brought him on from patient to therapist in the space of a couple of days!"

Stevie blew on her perfectly lacquered nails and polished them on the lapel of her jacket. "Well, you always knew I was good, didn't you?" She smiled then looked more serious. "He's a special man. He has a lot to offer. And not just sexually. It takes strength of character to come through what he's come through and remain so well adjusted. I really think he's just what Renata needs."

The doctor fell silent, but a kind of communication passed between them nevertheless. Hettie felt a pang of intense guilt. The relationship symmetry at Dragonwood suddenly seemed to exclude her beautiful friend. Twos into five did not go, and wise, experienced Stevie was taking herself out of the field of play.

"But, Stevie, please. I wanted you to have a nice little holiday. A chance to chill out," she still protested.

"And I have had. It's been wonderful," Stevie affirmed, her green eyes steady. "But I'm a fifth wheel here now, and my secretary's just rung about a couple of emergency appointments. I need to be back in London, love."

Obviously, Stevie had commitments, and Hettie accepted that, but she was still going to miss her daring friend. And it must have shown on her face.

"Don't worry, Hett," said Stevie reassuringly. "Darryl and Renata will be fine. And so will you and Starr. Trust me."

"I want to believe you, Stevie. And part of me does. But it's slow going. Sometimes I think we're almost there, and he's going to say something…then blam, we're back to square one again!"

"That's because you've got to make the first move," Stevie said emphatically. "It's all there inside him, love, but there's a wall in front of it that you've got to break down." She grinned suddenly. "And I don't mean something so antifeminist as crawling to him, woman… You've just got to tell him! And if he insists on adhering to this demented 'servant' stance of his, you've simply got to order him to admit it!"

"Admit what?"

"That he loves you, of course, twit!" Stevie laughed softly, then gave Hettie a quick, hard hug.

"Hang in there, sweetheart, it'll happen," the doctor whispered, and pressed a kiss to Hettie's cheek. Then she leapt to her feet, flipped an elegant little salute and said, "See you back in London. Good luck! And phone me to let me know what happens!"

And with that, the good doctor swept from the room and closed the door firmly behind her.

"Bye, Stevie," whispered Hettie. Weird thoughts drifted through her mind again for a moment. Thoughts about what might have been if there had been no Starr in the world. But they were only notions, as fleeting as images glimpsed through the window of a speeding car.

A short while later, as Hettie was completing her toilette, there was another knock.

More "what if"?

Hettie made sure her robe was covering everything and her sash tightly tied. It hadn't been Starr's firm decisive knock, but one much more tentative.

Caller number two *was* Darryl, and Hettie stifled a sigh of appreciation. She was throwing him together with his probably less than deserving cousin now, but she still had to admit he was a prime piece of eye candy. He looked sensational in a pair of white tennis shorts and a racer-back shirt that highlighted his delicious Mediterranean coloring.

"So, Darryl, what can I do for you at this time of the morning?" It came out sounding a tiny bit more suggestive than she'd intended and he smiled shyly in response. It was sweet that he could still be so bashful after his display on the patio yesterday with Stevie.

"I was going to bring you some tea, but Stevie said she'd

bring it," he began hesitantly. "What I really wanted was to talk though."

"Yes, and I think I know what about," she said encouragingly, patting the bed at her side. "I've had a pep talk from Stevie too. About what *I* ought to do." She paused and bit her lip. "And whom I ought to be doing it with."

"Oh," he said softly.

"And I think she's right really, don't you?"

He nodded and there was a long quiet moment while he seemed to gather his thoughts.

"Renata's not strong like you are, Hettie," he said at last. "She needs someone to take charge and I think that if I become that someone it'll make *me* strong."

He took a twist of the bedspread in his long tawny fingers and started worrying it. "I like Ren and I think I could a lot more than like her when we really get to know each other. *Dio*, I'm not putting this very well, am I?"

"It's okay. I understand, Darryl, don't worry."

"He's down by the river, I think." Darryl accompanied his sudden change of tack with a smile and Hettie smiled too, no longer scared by his uncanny intuition. "I saw him set off in that direction a short while ago... And he looked as if he was thinking some very deep thoughts."

"He's not the only one!" she said, laughing softly. "Now go and give Renata the benefit of everything you've learnt in the last few days!"

"With the greatest of pleasure," Darryl answered, giving her a wicked wink and blowing her a kiss before disappearing out of the door.

"I'm sure it will be," whispered Hettie as she jumped up and began to hunt around for something to wear. Something that wasn't black.

"Well, Piers, how do you like it?" she asked, standing at the bottom of the stairs, dressed in white, in front of a portrait of her late husband.

It could've been wishful thinking, but Piers seemed to wink at her and approve what she was about to do.

It was all your idea anyway, wasn't it, my love?

Smiling to herself, she stepped out of the door into a beautiful morning. She'd been set up, she decided, just as Stevie had said. But as she watched the trees by the river swaying gently in the breeze, she accepted that she didn't mind Piers' machinations at all. Not one little bit. Down in that leafy grove was where Starr was, thinking his thoughts and pondering their future, and suddenly she wanted to be there too.

The sun was warm on Hettie's legs as she ran down the steps, past the glinting pool and out through the tiered garden towards the grass. What would Starr think of this outfit, these clothes she'd scavenged from the wardrobe she'd left behind the last time she'd stayed here with Piers? White shorts—very short shorts!—white T-shirt and neat white deck shoes. And beneath, tiny white panties that were already beginning to get moist.

She paused when she reached the edge of the formal garden and looked up towards the balcony and the row of bedroom windows. The curtains of the window of Renata's room were still drawn to and Hettie hoped with all her heart that behind them something wonderful was happening.

For all her follies and foolishness, Ren was a sweet girl and she deserved some happiness after all the false starts she'd had with the men in her life. And Darryl had everything necessary to make her happy. Beauty, gentleness, a kind, caring disposition and probably—even after only a couple of days tuition—a precocious talent in bed. With the enthusiastic and intuitive Signor di Angeli between her thighs, Hettie doubted if Renata would have problems with orgasms for much longer!

You're lucky I'm spoken for, Ren!

Heart happy, Hettie broke into a run again, devouring the greensward of the park at an almost competitive speed in her haste to reach the trees, the river…and her destiny.

Sunlight on water twinkled through the copse as she entered it, heading for the place where the small river widened into a semblance of a pool. There was a fallen tree in a clearing there, a kind of natural bench where she'd once—while exploring—happened on a certain tall blond blue-eyed man engaged in some sketching. He hadn't allowed her to see his work, of course, and had covered the page immediately, then distracted her attention by pointing out a kingfisher about to dart into the stream.

As she cut silently amongst the trees, her footsteps masked by moss and soft undergrowth, she could see him. Sitting on his log, the dappled sunlight glinting on his naked back as he bent over the drawing pad spread across his parted thighs. His concentration seemed total, but knowing Starr as she did, it seemed impossible that he wasn't aware of her approach.

Finally, she stopped just a couple of feet away from where he sat, but he still didn't look up or turn.

It seemed ludicrous to be afraid of speaking to this man she'd made love with so many times, but Hettie's heart was in her mouth and any words she might have said had suddenly dried up.

"Good morning, ma'am," he said quietly, his pencil

gliding over the smooth white paper.

"Good morning, Starr," she answered, stepping closer. "May I see what you're drawing?"

"Of course." He paused in his work and edged along the tree trunk, making space for her to sit beside him.

The sketch wasn't at all what she'd expected. Instead of a woodland view, the paper bore a very detailed and finely worked sketch of a face and body she knew only too well…

A naked figure, gracefully reclining and eyes closed as if sleeping. A woman utterly relaxed after lovemaking. It was herself, Lady Henrietta Miller, posed amongst the tangled sheets in her bedroom at Pengilley Gardens. And drawn entirely from memory.

"I don't know what to say," she whispered, her throat suddenly thick with tears. "You've made me look beautiful."

"You *are* beautiful, milady." He yielded up the pad as she tugged it onto her own lap for a better look. Peripherally, she registered that he too seemed to have decided it was time to dispense with black clothing. His long muscular thighs disappeared into a pair of ragged blue denim cutoffs. It was his only garment and his feet were as bare as his gleaming upper body.

"Oh my," she muttered as she flipped over page after page, drawing after drawing, every single one a likeness of her. His talent and technical expertise were undeniable but it was the raw emotion in every line that took her breath away.

"But why?" she demanded, flipping the pad closed, dazzled by the intensity of what she'd seen and the fire that burned beneath the familiar images of her body and face.

"Because I can't stop myself," he said simply.

For a moment, Hettie didn't know what to say or do. To draw her over and over again obsessively must mean what she hoped it meant but she was still scared that she was hoping for too much. Screwing up her courage, she put the drawing pad down on the grass next to the log, then reached up and took the pencil from Starr's still fingers and dropped it with the pad.

"Look, I don't know how to say this... How to ask..." She faltered. "But I know I've got to because if I don't you might never ask me!"

She sensed him tense beside her and her fear swirled up, tightening in her throat and pounding in her chest. But she'd begun so she had to go on.

"Starr, please tell me. I know we've made love... So many times... But what do you *really* think about me? Do you have any feelings for me of your own? Other than duty and loyalty to Piers? Please, I need a straight answer!"

It sounded so childish, like the questions posed by little girls in their playground cliques. *Do you like me? Do you want to be on my side?* Wishing she'd never asked at all she looked straight up into a pair of eyes that were clear as the water beside them but blue as the mightiest of oceans.

He didn't grimace or scowl, but he didn't smile either. Hettie shook. After what seemed like a lifetime, he pursed his lips. Then his eyelashes flicked down once and he spoke.

"I love you, ma'am," he said with quiet dignity. "I've loved you from the first instant I set eyes on you. You were standing in the doorway of a gallery in Mayfair, holding Sir Piers' arm." His voice faded away almost, and ocean blue turned dark and stormy.

"You'd just met and I had to drive you to his house so the two of you could make love for the first time."

Hettie felt a huge pain savage her, and knew she was feeling only the faintest echo of what the man beside her had felt. "He was going to possess you. Make love with you. Take what I suddenly wanted more than anything in the world."

His knuckles were clenched, white against the strong sinewy gold of his hands. "There, milady, is that straight enough for you?"

She felt anger fizzing out of him and knew that it was not the first time he'd felt it. She hardly dare think about the suffering he'd gone through for her. Lovemaking must have been as much a torment for him as a pleasure if he was entrenched in the belief that he was merely an employee performing a particularly intimate service.

"Thank you, Starr. Thank you for your honesty," she said, grabbing at every ounce of her boldness and reaching out to take his hands and smooth the tension from his fingers. "It deserves a straight answer."

No hesitation now, Hettie!

"I loved Piers, and I still love him. I don't think I'll ever stop. But that doesn't mean I can't love others too. I've become fond of Darryl. And I certainly care for Stevie…" Gripping his hand, she raised it to her lips and kissed it quickly before her courage failed her. "But you… I *love* you, Starr. I can't put my hand on my heart and say exactly when it happened, but it's been around for quite a while."

The next silence lasted for a thousand lifetimes. A millennium. An eon. Until Starr smiled. "That's wonderful, ma'am," he said softly.

"I'm glad you think so," she answered pertly as her confidence came storming back and brought a tidal wave of arousal with it. She'd have to have him in her soon or she'd pass out, but there was still one last detail to finalize.

"And that means there's another thing I've got to ask. Because I can't see *you* asking it in a hurry."

He quirked his fine and surprisingly dark eyebrows in sudden amusement, then reached out and put one long finger across her lips, effectively silencing her.

"Will you marry me, milady?"

Hettie gasped as he withdrew the fingertip. For a moment she felt light-headed with joy. All the unspoken dreams and wishes that had been gathering slowly but surely had come to perfect fulfillment in the space of a heartbeat.

"Well?" She saw a momentary flash of doubt darken his amazing, sculpted features, and wanted to kiss away the slight frown on his brow. Kiss away every doubt he'd ever had and ever would have for all the future that lay ahead of them…

"Of course, Starr," she said, at a loss for anything else.

"Good, I thought you might," he said, his face perfectly straight again. And so deliciously smug she could almost have slapped him.

"What? You don't think it's inappropriate, improper or 'not your place' then?" she inquired, feeling delirious enough to tease him.

"No, not now." The expression on his face grew serious again for a moment. "I've been a coward too long… Hiding behind a convenient role. Afraid of fighting for what I want."

Then the seriousness faded, and his sensuous lips curved into a warm, devilish smile. "But now I've decided to stop being a fool. And kick out all the stupid restrictions I placed on myself… Because I was the one who put them there. It was never Piers…or you." He paused, then looked at her very levelly. "I think that us getting married is an excellent idea."

"Is that a fact?" she shot back, grinning and deciding that she'd never met a *less* cowardly or foolish man in her life. "Well, now we've got that sorted out, do you think you could possibly manage to make love to me?"

He could more than manage, she could see that. Beneath the denim of his shorts, his erection was already pushing and rising.

"Of course, ma'am," he said solemnly, his blue eyes alight with laughter and what she could see quite clearly now was love.

"Kindly get on with it then."

He didn't say "of course, ma'am" again but it was there in his handsome face, the way he bit his lip and rolled his eyes as if it were an effort *not* to say it. Instead of words he let his actions speak, swiveling his hands out of her grip, then taking hold of her by the shoulders and drawing her up alongside him as he got to his feet.

Starr was so tall and so straight that he had to bend down to kiss her on the mouth. He took her lips with the most feather-light gentleness, stroking their outline with his tongue and then with the merest of pressures, asking for entrance and acceptance. Hettie gave it gladly, receiving his heat and moisture with the happiest of hearts, her mouth, her body and very soul opening to him as his steely arms closed around her.

It was the most romantic of kisses, their mouths moving softly on one another to the sound of rippling water and rustling branches and birdsong. And yet it was sexual too. Sexy in the tasting, the rhythmic exchange of tongue thrusts, the moisture that flowed between them and anew between Hettie's legs. Most of all, it was erotic in the rubbing of their groins against each other—she circling her pubis against the unyielding muscle of his thigh, and he, the taller one, pressing his potent erection against her soft cotton-clad belly.

Who was teasing whom the most? Hettie wondered. She was enjoying these preliminaries, but suddenly she wanted control. She wanted to be in charge of this lovemaking, not just the recipient of Starr's great skill as she so often was.

Reaching between them she sought and found the button

on his shorts, then slipped it open. Not releasing his mouth from the kiss, she reached inside the shabby denim garment and discovered to her joy that he was naked underneath it. His cock almost leaped into her grasp, its tip wet and silky while the shaft was hotter and harder than she'd ever felt it before. As she fondled him, she felt him release her for a second or two then push down his shorts so that they fell in a heap around his ankles.

What a drawing this would make, she thought, flicking her tongue around the inside of his mouth as she delicately masturbated the swollen head of his cock.

The two of them standing in a woodland glade, she clothed and he nude and golden and submitting to the most intimate of handling while he kissed her. She could feel the groans rising in his throat as she pressed and probed at the most sensitive areas of his cock, squeezing the glans and spreading his slippery pre-come all over the fine satin skin that almost seared her fingers with its heat.

Fondling him mercilessly, she sucked at his tongue like a famished beast, timing the swirls of her own tongue with the tantalizing play of her fingertips along the sensitive undergroove of his cock head. He wanted to shout and moan, she knew it, but there was no way she was going to free his mouth until he'd spent in her hand.

He was fighting it. Always having been strong for her, she guessed that giving in like this was alien to his independent and dominant nature. But she *would* have this! She would have him climax at her touch, at her command. Slipping her free hand around his back, she pressed one finger, then two into his anus. He was relaxed, his sexual focus elsewhere, and she was able to slide in deeply and easily.

She felt him buck against her, both in shock and in pleasure, and she drew as hard on his tongue as she could and twisted and waggled her fingers.

With his tongue thrashing in her mouth, she caressed the inside of his rectum and within seconds his cock pulsed heavily and semen spurted out of its tip. Hettie made a fist around his glans and contained the rich and luscious fluid in the cradle of her fingers. It was hers, just as *he* was hers, and neither would ever escape her again.

As his shaking body stilled and he stood up straight between her possession of his cock and his anus, Hettie lowered her mouth and kissed the hard-packed muscle of his chest.

"Thank you, my lady," he said quietly as she released him and gave him back his power. Or at least some of it.

"I haven't finished with you, mister," she murmured as she stepped back and began to undress herself. "Lie down over there," she said, pointing to a slight hollow in the turf some few feet away, a moss-lined indentation which would make a perfect natural bed for them.

With a grace that took her breath away, he complied, placing his body like some ancient Greek athlete or god, the glorious lines of his limbs as acutely desirable to her as the cock that was already regaining its stiffness.

It took her just thirty seconds to shuck off her own clothes and lie down beside him. He reached for her immediately, his fingers temptingly warm and sure, but she rolled just out of his reach.

"No, no. Not yet," she whispered, kneeling up and coming over him again, holding down his hands as she let her mouth taste what her fingers had already pleasured. Her hair curtained down over his thighs as she took the head of his cock between her lips.

She didn't suck hard. A quick flood of semen wasn't what she wanted. Licking him very gently, she simply said "hello again" to the bloated tip of him and prodded her tongue gently into the tiny slit.

His cry—"Oh God!"—was barely out of his mouth when she backed off again and sent her lips on a voyage of discovery—a slow, slow exploration of every part of him that enchanted her. In the filtered, piebald light of their forest bedchamber, she set out to kiss every inch of his long, golden body.

For a full half an hour, she caressed him with her mouth. She licked and nuzzled and tasted, covering the whole of the front of him with silky wet kisses, then making him turn over so she could continue her adoration across his back, his buttocks and his anus. When she kissed him there, probing wickedly with her tongue, she thought she'd gone too far. He groaned loudly, his thighs and torso shaking as if he were about to orgasm violently. But then, with what seemed like a supreme effort of will, he steadied his body and calmly accepted her tongue.

As she pulled away, and then pushed at his shoulder to turn him over again, Hettie knew that the time for teasing was over. Knowing it was ever her fate, she lay back on the moss, opened her wet thighs wide and touched a forefinger to her flowing sex in silent invitation.

Starr lay beside her for a few seconds, as if gathering himself, then slowly and with great elegance, he moved across and slotted himself effortlessly between her legs.

Swimming with moisture, her body accepted him with exquisite ease. Her channel was his natural home and nothing seemed more right and fitting than for him to be deep inside her.

After what had just passed between them, Hettie had expected to start thrusting straight away. She was within seconds of orgasm and it would only take a couple of strokes.

But Starr was not as other men, and with a great wash of joy, she realized that on *this* as on most other occasions, she should have expected the unexpected.

Adjusting her beneath him, he cupped her buttocks and tilted her pelvis in his hands so that his cock could slide in even deeper. It seemed the most wonderful thing in the world to comply with this, lifting her legs and locking her ankles behind his hips so his glans could slide right in and caress the neck of her womb. They were as close as a man and woman could ever be now, his cock as far inside her as it could get. With a sigh of mutual contentment, they settled into perfect stillness.

"Can I ask you something, Starr?" she whispered into his ear, squeezing him with her inner muscles and getting a gasp of pleasure in response.

"Yes, milady," he murmured, his voice catching when she squeezed him again.

"It's two things actually." It was her turn to gasp when he swirled his hips and his penis seemed to swivel inside her. "The first is… Oh God! The first is… Do you think you could start calling me Hettie *all* the time, now we're going to be married?"

She felt him breathe it against her ear and her heart felt fit to burst with happiness. "That's better… And I do mean *all* the time, not just when you're in me," she purred.

"Of course, M—" He chuckled and the laugh translated itself into a glorious vibration right at the core of her. "Of course, Hettie my love."

"The other thing is…" She pressed her mouth quickly to his neck, knowing that orgasm would not be held off much longer. Just lying still with him was as exciting as the wildest of sexual acrobatics with anyone else. "When you're my husband I'll need to call you by your first name. Do you think you could possibly tell me what it is?"

He laughed again and her climax came floating closer. "You'll laugh, Hettie."

"No, I won't! Believe me…" She was almost coming now. It was only curiosity—the unbearable need to know—that kept her from orgasming spontaneously.

"You *will* laugh," he assured her gently, pausing to kiss her throat. "You most certainly will laugh, I promise you." He paused again, slipping a hand between them and tapping his own chest for emphasis. "*My* first name, my dearest, darling *Henrietta* is"— he hesitated again, teasingly— "*Henry!*"

Lady Henrietta Miller did laugh then. She couldn't stop laughing. She laughed and laughed and laughed until the moment when her laughter turned to cries of joyous ecstasy and she climaxed like a chain of firecrackers around the strong pounding cock of her future husband.

Her beloved Henry Starr…

Thank You!

Many thanks for reading **Lessons and Lovers**.
I do hope you enjoyed Hettie and Starr and their erotic journey towards true love. And also Darryl's voyage of sensual enlightenment too.
Reviews are a wonderful way to help other readers find books, so please do consider reviewing **Lessons and Lovers** at Amazon, Goodreads, or at your favourite site of choice.
I appreciate all reviews I receive.

About Portia Da Costa

Portia Da Costa is a *New York Times*, *USA Today* and *Sunday Times* best-selling British author of romance, erotic romance and erotica, whose short stories and novels have been published in the UK and elsewhere since 1991. She loves creating stories about sexy, likeable people in steamy, scandalous situations, and has written for various publishers over the years, including Black Lace, HQN, Spice Briefs, Samhain Publishing, Carina Press and a good many others. Though her best known titles are mainly contemporary erotic romance, she also enjoys writing super hot Victorian historical romance, and erotic paranormals. She's even turned her hand to a bit of erotic sci-fi and horror on occasion.

When her Black Lace contemporary erotic romance IN TOO DEEP reached Number #5 in the *Sunday Times* paperback fiction chart only books by E L James and Sylvia Day were outselling her!

When Portia isn't writing she's usually to be found relaxing around the house, watching television or reading a wide variety of fiction and non fiction. She lives in the heart of West Yorkshire in the UK, with her husband and their four beloved cats, Mork, Mindy, Felix and Prince.

Discover more about Portia at **www.portiadacosta.com** or find her on Twitter, Facebook and Pinterest.

Erotic and Sensual Romance published by Portia Da Costa

AN APPOINTMENT WITH HER MASTER

ANOTHER APPOINTMENT

DARING INTERLUDES

DELICIOUS PAIN

EROTIC ESCAPADES

FIRE AND ICE

FORBIDDEN TREASURES

GLINT

HER SECRET

HIS SECRET

IN SEBASTIAN'S HANDS

LESSONS AND LOVERS

NAUGHTY THOUGHTS

POWER OF THREE

TEMPTED BY TWO

THE EFFICIENCY EXPERT

THEIR SECRET

WESLEY AND THE SEX ZOMBIES

Recent Black Lace and Harlequin Titles by Portia Da Costa

THE ACCIDENTAL CALL GIRL

THE ACCIDENTAL MISTRESS

THE ACCIDENTAL BRIDE

HOW TO SEDUCE A BILLIONAIRE

MASTER OF THE GAME

THE RED COLLECTION

THE STRANGER

IN TOO DEEP

IN THE FLESH

A GENTLEWOMAN'S QUARTET

DISCIPLINE OF THE BLUE BOOK

RITUAL OF THE RED CHAIR

ECSTASY IN THE WHITE ROOM